THE
BOY
WHO
LOVED
DOLPHINS

THE BOY WHO LOVED DOLPHINS

By Rob G. Lerner

Cover by PJ Hines

Pomanjer Publishing Co., LLC

Copyright

Pomanjer Publishing

E-book publication 2012
ISBN 978-0-615-69784-0

Print publication 2020
ISBN 978-0-9992511-7-1

About the Publisher

Pomanjer Publishing Co., LLC, focuses on books that spark curiosity in all genres, fiction and nonfiction.

About the book:

The Boy Who Loved Dolphins
By Rob G. Lerner
Cover by PJ Hines

Timmy is a young boy who feels alienated from his mother and stepfather. He gravitates toward his aging and beloved grandfather, who fills his head with wild fantasies of life beneath the sea. When his grandfather suddenly dies, Timmy feels adrift, and when his family takes a vacation on the North Carolina coast, he tries to remain close to his grandfather by living out some of the old man's fantasies. Things take a strange turn when Timmy turns into a dolphin, and a group of wild dolphins adopt him. Ocean life should be as wonderful as his grandfather promised, but Timmy quickly realizes that fantasies are a poor substitute for family, friends, or his grandfather.

About the Author

Rob G. Lerner was born in California and resides in Virginia with his wife and son (who always gets to go to the beach on the first day of vacation). Rob has been crafting fiction for years, although this is his only book that features animals and supernatural events. Rob will soon be publishing his next book. Follow Rob's literary progress, leave review comments on this and his other books, and contact Rob through:
https://www.amazon.com/author/robglerner

Also by Rob G. Lerner

Changers
Minders
Snapshot
The Nesbit Bunch
The Resurrection of the Father

To Alex

Contents

I

It was the largest book that he had ever seen. It was half as tall as he was and nearly as thick as his outspread hand. And it was heavy. It was probably the heaviest thing that he had ever owned, if not the biggest, and he struggled with it every time he pulled it out from under his bed, which was practically the only place he could put it to ensure its safety. However, it wasn't the size of the book that pleased him, although there was something to the size that filled him with outsized expectations. No, it was what was inside, and inside the book was picture after picture of dolphins - - dolphins swimming in the sea, dolphins jumping out of the sea, dolphins jumping in and jumping out of the sea, as well as pictures of young dolphins, old dolphins, and baby dolphins.

Timmy loved dolphins. Even before he got the book and had seen the aquarium for himself, Timmy was in love with dolphins in all their infinite variety, and now that he owned this gigantic book, he loved them even more. He loved their smooth, silver lines, and the effortless way they had of moving in and out of the water, practically floating wherever they went. And he loved their happy, smiling faces. He loved that most of all. Timmy had never seen animals, much less human beings, so filled with the joy of life that they could not suppress their smiles.

The book had been a gift from his grandfather. 'Grandpa,' a heavyset old man with a large stomach, unkempt gray hair, and several days of facial hair on his flabby jowls, had lugged the book into the house all by himself when he visited the family last year, which sadly turned out to be only a few months before his death. Timmy didn't look a thing like his Grandpa – he was eight years old, slim, and had a mop of brown hair that hung over his eyebrows – but he wished he did, for he loved his Grandpa more than anyone else in the world. The old man had never failed to send him cards and gifts – never once forgetting his birthday or Christmas – and, more importantly, he was always smiling, just like a dolphin, at least when he looked at Timmy. Timmy loved his visits, which occurred like clockwork every four months, because they filled the house with excitement in a way that probably only a dolphin could generate. Timmy would never forget the last time his Grandpa had been able to take him some place, or how the old man had peremptorily informed his mother that he was taking Timmy to the aquarium and would be back later in the afternoon.

The day was unusually warm, and for most of the morning the sky had been clear and bright. Timmy was in the house, eating lunch in the kitchen, when he heard his Grandpa and his mom heatedly discussing something.

"I can't believe he's never been to the aquarium," the old man was saying, as he and Tommy's mother stood face to face in the center of the living room. Timmy quietly watched them, peering around the corner while Bob, his stepfather, cleaned and put away the dishes. "That boy loves marine life, and he should be there right now, watching and learning from the fish with someone who loves him, like I do. The boy needs attention, and I cannot fathom why you don't understand this. He needs someone to take him places, someone to support his interests, someone to show him the same love and attention that your mother and I showed you. I don't understand why if you won't spare the time that I can't…"

"Enough," she said firmly. "I am tired of hearing the same nonsense over and over. I'm an unfit mother, Bob's not his father, and neither Bob nor I love Timmy like you do. Oh, and I forgot. You hate your apartment. The old women there are continually sneaking into your apartment and stealing your things. And…what am I leaving out? Yes, you don't have any friends because the residents there are abominable. Do I have it right? Have I missed anything? Well, let me add this, since the subject is likely to come up even if you don't mention it directly – I am not going to say another word about Tom. Never again. I'm sorry I married him, and I am sorry the damned fool got drunk, staggered into the neighbor's pool, and drowned. Now, have we covered everything? Oh," she sighed, shaking her head. "I shouldn't have to say this, but I do a lot of things with Timmy, every chance I get, and so does Bob. You can't imagine how good Bob is to that boy…"

2

"I can imagine. But you haven't been to the aquarium – I'll bet Bob hasn't taken him to the aquarium – and it's been there for how many years? Name a single thing that you've done with Timmy since my last visit, or even in the past six months?"

"We've done plenty of things. Besides, it's none of your business. Let me tell you this, I am a good mother despite – or maybe in spite of – all your interference, and I resent the insinuation that just because we haven't been to the fish place, I am somehow a bad mother because of it. Look," she continued, her voice increasing and her face becoming red, "I am tired of hearing you say that I am a...an unfit human being. I've done a lot of things with Timmy, but I haven't had a chance to go to the aquarium recently because life is busy sometimes..."

"Have you explained to him that he can't go to the aquarium because 'life is busy sometimes...'?"

"It's easy for you to say that, because you have all the free time in the world and...," she snapped, and then evidently had a change of heart because her tone suddenly softened. "I'd like to take him some time. I'd like to take him to a lot of places, but it isn't always easy to find the time. Both Bob and I work, and Timmy has to go to school....and, don't say it, we do have weekends and holidays, but we are usually engaged in other things, often with and for him. But what you don't understand is that he can sometimes be difficult for one person to handle. Even with both of us, it's hard. I know, it's not the same with you – he's as sweet as a pea with you -- but that little pea has a bad habit of running off the second my back is turned. I don't know what it is with that boy (and, believe me, I've spoken to him about running away enough times to make your head spin), but I have to tell you that some times I am afraid of taking him places, afraid that he's going to do something stupid and end up like..." She hesitated, before continuing. "You have a pleasant, uncomplicated life in your community. I know, I know, the people there aren't what you had in mind, but what is so bad about living there? Do the women there really steal things, or is that just another one of your stories?"

3

"Talking like that doesn't hurt me…"

"I'm sorry," she replied, no longer angry and sorry that she had said something that was certain to hurt the old man's feelings. "I shouldn't have said that."

"You've got a wonderful son who needs attention, and it's a mother's job to give him that attention while watching over him…"

"He gets plenty of attention, from both me and Bob…and you. Look, I've made mistakes, and so have you, but life isn't about perfection. I am doing the best I can, Bob and I are doing the best we can, and so for once will you please stop…"

The old man stared at his daughter for a moment, as if he couldn't quite understand what she was saying, and then, frowning, abruptly turned around and marched into an adjoining room, where he plopped himself into a soft, oversized chair, picked up an old magazine that had been lying on the floor and began to read.

Timmy's mother folded her arms and remained standing, as if she were waiting for the old man to return. When, after a few moments, he didn't, she stomped her right foot softly on the floor, dropped her arms to her sides, and followed him into the other room.

"Why does it always have to be like this?" she demanded, standing in front of him and staring at the back of his magazine. He didn't reply, and calmly turned a page as if she wasn't there. She could feel her anger rising again, and while she was able to control herself, she was unable to hold back a familiar concern that had characterized their relations for some time. "I'm sorry. Can you understand me? Please, don't do this to me. Not again…"

The old man closed the magazine and carefully returned it to the floor, as if it were a precious object. Leaning back in his chair, he looked up at her and, with a blank expression on his face, replied, "You don't have to apologize to me. I am too old to need your apologies. But that wonderful boy of yours does. He's not an object that you can take from the shelf and play with only when it suits your purpose. He needs to be the focus of your busy life, and until this happens I fear that he will never get the attention he needs to grow up happy and well adjusted. I…"

"Please, can we stop this?" She closed her eyes briefly and sighed. "What do you want? Do you want to take him to the fish place, is that it?"

"Aquarium."

"Yes, the aquarium. Is that what's you're angling for?"

"Funny. But I'm only concerned about what's best for my grandson. I've never been concerned about anything else, not even those old women. I don't know why you can't see that."

The old man stared into her eyes, while she stared back, mulling something over in her mind. Fifteen minutes later, without another word between them, Timmy was waving to his mother out the window of a taxi that was taking him and Grandpa to the aquarium.

That night, long after everyone had gone to bed, Timmy dreamed about dolphins. He dreamed mainly about the dolphins that he had seen in the aquarium, although in one dream he was riding on the back of a large, silver dolphin that was swimming a hundred feet off shore. The sun was directly overhead and, because there were no clouds in the sky, it was oppressively hot and the beach glistened as if it were on fire. Timmy could see his Grandpa clearly. He was dressed in the same old, shabby clothes that he always wore – a baggy floral shirt with oversized pants and brown slippers – but he was sitting on a small red-striped towel beneath a large, red-striped umbrella and watching his grandson intently as he rode the beautiful dolphin back and forth across the horizon. It was evident from the old man's glistening tears, which were streaming down his shaggy cheeks, that he admired Timmy's skill, especially when he raised one hand above his head and waved to the old man while the dolphin leaped out of the water and plunged back under the surface. Moments later, when the dolphin burst back through the surface and sailed high into the air, Timmy was still securely sitting on the animal's shiny back, just as he had been when he first got on. His Grandpa's tears increased when, with a smile and another wave of his hand, Timmy turned the dolphin toward the open sea and disappeared into the golden light of the setting sun.

II

Three months after the bad news, one month after a tentative settlement, and one week before the last day of school, Timmy, his mother, and Bob piled into the family car and headed to a beach house on the North Carolina coast, which was about three hours away. "This is the first time that we've been able to get away in I don't know how long," Timmy's mother crooned several times throughout their drive. "Yes, it's been a long time, and I think we all deserve it," she added each time, as if to allay concerns regarding the timing of the trip.

"Timmy, you and I are going to…," Bob started to say at one point, but he didn't finish because he had to maneuver around a large pot hole in the road and lost his train of thought. Timmy hadn't been listening very carefully anyway, because he, too, was excited about the beach vacation, even though he was still sad over the passing of his Grandpa.

Timmy had never been to the beach before, and the sum total of his knowledge about the ocean had come from books, particularly his large dolphin book, and of course the trip to the aquarium that he had taken with his Grandpa. He tried to imagine what it would be like standing on the beach, his pants legs rolled up and the wet sand squishing between his toes, and looking out across the calm, blue water in search of dolphins. He would have to shield his eyes with his hands as the sun's rays bounced off the brilliant white sand, but neither that nor anything else could prevent him from spotting dolphins swimming and leaping in the water. 'They will be easy to see,' he assured himself, 'because the water is filled with them. Some of the dolphins might even swim close enough to shore to touch,' he added, closing his eyes and pretending to reach out and gently stroke the back of one such dolphin, which responded with a series of whistles and clicking sounds. In response to Timmy's question regarding how long they were going to stay, his mother said that they could stay as long as they liked or as long as they were having fun.

"We can't stay forever," Bob interjected, as they rolled into the driveway in front of the house late that afternoon. "Or at least I can't. I may have to go back to the office to clear up a few things."

The house looked like one of those old 19th century mansions you sometimes see in movies. Three stories high, it was crowned with several pointed gables (the highest was topped by a tall, black weather cock), and painted in a bright yellow, except for the shutters, which were a pale and peeling apple green and flanked every window. The overall appearance was warm and inviting, especially at that very moment as the sun slipped behind the houses across the street and cast a single golden ray on the house's highest gable, making everyone optimistic that they would have fun just like Timmy's mother promised. Unfortunately, even though the house was less than a block from the beach, the ocean wasn't visible because of the large sand dunes out back and the presence of some newly constructed houses a few yards to the left. The rental agent, though, assured Bob that at night when the air is still, one can hear the waves crashing against the beach and then washing across the sand up to the base of the dunes. "'Sounds like a distant cannon going off,'" Bob said, quoting the agent. Timmy's mother added that the man (meaning the agent) also said there was a chance that one could hear the whales as they made their way down the coast in search of food and warmer waters. "I wouldn't count on it," Bob replied, although addressing his comments to Timmy. "I don't think this is whale season."

Sadly, there was no chance of seeing whales or dolphins or anything else on the first day of their stay, because it was too late to go to the beach, his mother explained, and because they were all tired, Bob added. Besides, the evening paper reported a storm that was coming later that evening, which, Bob emphasized, "could last several days. I don't want you to get your hopes up of seeing the water right away. We'll see what happens." The paper was right about the storm. It hit shortly after dinner and continued through the night and into the early morning, rattling the windows and howling so insistently that it made sleep difficult and set everyone on edge. Luckily, the power stayed on most of the night, and after breakfast the sun was overhead, the sky was deep blue, and the remnants of the storm, a narrow streak of dark clouds, were barely visible on the horizon. As they stepped out onto the back deck shortly before lunch to look at the dunes, a warm breeze caressed their faces and filled their noses with the pleasant smell of sea water. In the distance they could hear the muffled boom of a cannon and then the hiss of the water racing across the sand, just as the agent had promised.

The beautiful morning filled Timmy with the hope that they would finally go to the beach. He was eager to feel the sand between his toes, to watch the warm foam rise and surround his legs, and to find seashells as the water retreated. More importantly, he wanted to see the dolphins. He knew what Bob had said about the whales, but he was certain that there were dolphins, thousands of them, just off the shore where anyone could see them jumping and slashing through the water. Timmy was determined to find them, and he was increasingly confident that they would swim close enough to him that he could reach out and caress their rubbery skin. During lunch, before he repeated his request to go to the beach, he had asked his mother if he could ride a dolphin if it came near the shore. It wasn't an entirely serious question (he only wanted to talk about dolphins), but no sooner had he uttered the words than he started to wonder if it was possible. 'And why not?' he asked himself. 'They are friendly and people do it all the time in aquarium.' He knew his Grandpa would have approved. Timmy's mother laughed at the idea, and, as she passed out grilled cheese sandwiches in her yellow and green sun dress, she added that dolphins were dangerous fish and could bite a child's arm off if he got too close. "No one should go near the water when those nasty things are about," she added, taking a seat next to Bob.

Bob glanced over the top of his reading glasses and then returned to his newspaper, which he began to read as soon as they came back inside. "I don't want you to get any ideas, young man," he said without looking up from the paper, "because you can't swim. You stay away from the beach without your mother or me. Besides," he continued, using his index finger to locate a passage in the paper, "there aren't any dolphins around here. I've been to this beach many times – my family used to vacation here when I was a boy – and I can assure you that there isn't a single dolphin within a hundred miles of this stretch of coast." Having read the section in question, he pulled out another section of the paper and began reading that, albeit with less care. "Sweetheart," he added while turning the page, "dolphins aren't fish. They won't bite anyone's arms off. I think you're confusing them with sharks."

"I never claimed to be an expert," his mother replied softly, holding her coffee cup in both hands and gently blowing on the liquid to cool it down. After a few seconds, she turned to Bob and whispered, "Darling, please don't correct me in front of the boy."

Timmy was disappointed that no one was interested in talking about dolphins; and he refused to accept Bob's judgment that there were no dolphins on the other side of the dunes. 'If there aren't any dolphins,' he reasoned, 'then why is there a restaurant in town named after a dolphin? And why are there so many things in this house with dolphins on them?' There was a small lamp in the living room that was shaped like a dolphin and had small, leaping dolphins along the edge of the lampshade. There was a painting in the same room, over the fireplace, portraying three dolphins swimming in the ocean – one poking its smiling face out of the water, one leaping into the air, and one returning to the water. Across the water was a large sand dune, which looked exactly like the one behind the house. "Okay," Timmy said, looking at Bob and then his mother, "when can we go to the beach?"

"My goodness, the storm just ended and you're ready to play in the sand," his mother responded, as if someone his age should have asked a more reasonable question. "We don't know what the water will be like. We'll think about it for later."

"When?"

"I don't know. Ask…"

"Maybe this afternoon," Bob said absently, as he now began scanning through his checkbook. After a couple of moments of silence, he closed the book and looked directly at Timmy. "Look, I've got some work to do first, and your mother has something to do, too, I suppose. There'll be plenty of time to go to the beach. I'll think about it and call you when we're ready. Okay?"

Timmy knew from the man's tone that it was useless to argue with him. "May I go outside, then?" he asked.

"If it's not one thing, it's another," his mother said, even though Timmy was not speaking to her.

"Yes, you can go outside," Bob responded, once again absorbed in his checkbook. "Stay in the front yard."

"That's right. We haven't checked out the backyard yet. There could be spiders and…what do you call those other things, dear?" his mother asked, turning to her husband.

"Just spiders."

"Okay, spiders." His mother smiled at Timmy as he left the table and proceeded out the front door. "Remember," she called after him, "don't go any farther without Mummy or Bob. Did you hear me?" she called out after the front door closed.

III

There wasn't much to the front yard. Most of it was covered with white gravel made from ground up seashells, and the rest was a combination of grayish non-descript dirt and weeds. It was clear that the owners of the house didn't lavish the same care on the front yard that they had on the inside of the house, which was filled with bowls of sea shells and amazing pictures of dolphins and boats. There were even slowly floating seagulls on the walls of the bathroom in the basement, which for some reason didn't impress his mother or Bob.

Timmy walked around the yard, moving from one corner to the next, looking for something, anything, that might be of interest. There were some nearly complete seashells beside the driveway, but these were the kinds of shells that one could see anywhere and, besides, they looked like they belonged to someone else, given the way they were stacked on top of one another. There were also some small mounds of sea gravel near the house, evidence of another child's efforts to pass the time in the front productively. Timmy stared down at the small mounds, which were not particularly interesting, and then with the toe of his sandal, he smoothed out one of the mounds. There was a small stick nearby, and Timmy picked up the stick, weighed it carefully in his hand, and began to draw a picture.

At first, he drew some lines without trying to make any particular shape, but he quickly erased those because they weren't very interesting and he didn't care whether they lasted or not. Timmy was about to toss the stick and continue his exploration of the yard when it occurred to him that he could use the stick to draw a nice picture of the ocean. After all, it was the first day on the beach and, just as the agent had promised, he could hear the faint boom of the ocean beyond the dunes, or at least he thought he could hear it. A lot that it mattered, though. Stick in hand, poised to draw a more concrete image, he hesitated because he realized that the ocean could be on the moon for all anyone cared. No one was interested in seeing the water, and with his luck it could be days (if ever) before he got a chance to roll in the sand, splash in the waves, or scan the horizon for dolphins. He had no doubt that the dolphins were there now, waiting to demonstrate their tricks and skills, but he was considerably less confident that they would remain there until his mom and Bob got around to taking him to the beach – at any moment, they might move to another beach, leaving him wondering if they did the same tricks as aquarium dolphins or if they would have been happy to see him. Shaking his head to erase the unhappy thoughts from his mind, he began to draw in the loose sand, carefully moving his stick back and forth to form the exact shapes he needed.

Once Timmy finished drawing the ocean, he placed the sun and its rays in the upper right portion of the picture, where they were supposed to be, and then stepped back two steps to look at his creation. One thick line defined the horizon, while small curly lines denoted the waves below and clouds above the line. It was a pleasant image, although it would have been better had he been able to use his crayons to color in the water and clouds. But as he looked more closely at the picture, it occurred to him that something was missing, something that he couldn't immediately put his finger on. He tried adding two seagulls floating in the sky, but because they each looked like a floating "m," they messed up the sky and were clearly not what was needed. Irritated, Timmy once again used his toe to smooth out the dirt and erase his picture.

Timmy turned to go back inside the house when it dawned on him that what the picture needed was a dolphin. How could he have forgotten a dolphin? This time Timmy smoothed out a wider area of the dirt with his toe and went back to work. With the stick, he carefully inscribed the horizon and the sun, and then before adding anything else he began to outline a large dolphin that was jumping out of the water. The animal's nose and most of its body were reaching out of the water, while its tail was still submerged, ready to leave the water in less than a second. Timmy stood back and looked at his creation. The lines were not quite right and the images were missing color – and there was still something wrong about the sky -- but overall it satisfied him enough that he was ready to leave it and go on to something else.

But as he considered the picture one last time, it occurred to him that one dolphin might not be enough – why shouldn't there be two dolphins or even twenty? -- and so he etched another one in the picture, one that had left the confines of the water and was soaring through the sky, and then another one – this one had just passed from the sky to the water and was now swimming well below the surface, deep within the very heart of the ocean. The result was beautiful, much better than it had been with only one dolphin; and, despite the absence of color, Timmy was certain that if his mom and Bob cared to look, they would have understood the importance of dolphins in his life and the urgency of going to the beach before it was too late. He was also certain that had he been able to show his Grandpa the image, he would have found a way of preserving it and using it to keep Timmy in his heart, even when he was far away at his terrible apartment.

Thinking about his Grandpa made Timmy sad, and he longed to see him just as much as he longed to see a dolphin. For a few moments, tears welled up in his eyes, and then, once his eyes cleared, he smoothed out another area in the dirt next to his picture and drew a picture of his Grandpa looking at his drawing of the ocean and the dolphins. Only one thing remained at this point – Timmy added himself in the dolphin picture, riding the back of the dolphin soaring through the air.

Timmy ran back into the house and asked Bob, who was still at the kitchen table and now entering information from his checkbook into a computer, when they could go to the beach.

"Later," he said without looking up. "Probably not today. I thought I told you not to ask me again."

Timmy found his mother in one of the upstairs bedrooms, unpacking their clothes and struggling with a dresser drawer that had been inserted crookedly.

"Can we go to the beach today?" he asked cheerfully, hoping that she had not heard his discussion with Bob.

"Can't you see that I am busy?" she responded half mad at the dresser and half mad at him. "Would you like to do some work for a change? It's about time, young man. I could certainly use some help around here." When the drawer finally gave way and closed, she turned and stared at him, keeping her hands on her hips. "If you're not going to help me, I suppose you can go outside and play. Stay in the front yard and, for heaven's sake, please quit asking me those silly questions."

"Would you like to see the picture I made?"

"Later."

"Can I watch TV?"

"You can play quietly in your room or go outside."

"But there isn't anything to do. Don't you want to see my picture?"

"Timothy, you can either play outside or I will give you something to do. Now, please, I am busy."

"We're never going to see the dolphins," Timmy said dejectedly as he walked out of the room.

"Bob said there weren't any dolphins in these waters," he heard his mother call out after him as he walked out the front door and down the steps to the front yard. "Are you listening to me? Timothy?"

IV

Timmy considered himself a good child. He did his homework on time, he rarely left toys lying around where someone could step on them, and he almost never went anywhere without first getting permission. He didn't understand why his mom had told Grandpa that he ran away all the time when that was hardly ever the case. Certainly, he wasn't perfect, and there were times when he may have got lost, but for the most part he obeyed the rules, especially those that Bob established.

Today, however, was one of those days that pushed his obedience to its limits, for the prospect of whiling away the day in a barren front yard or, worse, playing quietly in his room was beyond endurance, especially after he had been promised a fun time at the beach, the very first beach he had ever seen. But as if this weren't bad enough, he was missing the dolphins. Timmy had no doubt that there were dolphins off the beach, and he couldn't stand the idea that he was stuck here, at this strange house, and forced to forgo perhaps the one real opportunity he would ever have of seeing dolphins in the wild. Who knows if he would ever again get a chance to see dolphins in the ocean? Maybe, he considered, Bob's statements that there weren't any dolphins at this beach reflected his own missed opportunities, not the absence of the dolphins.

Timmy looked down at the picture that he had drawn in the dirt and noticed that the lines delineating the dolphins were beginning to blur. It was not hard to imagine that the shapes would soon disappear, leaving nothing but a lifeless patch of dirt and rocks to be trampled on without the least regret. "If I don't see them now," he thought, "I may never see them before they move on to another beach or swim out into the open sea." Tears welled up into his eyes at the thought of missing these magnificent creatures, especially because he might never again have such a splendid opportunity.

Timmy was a little uneasy about his plan, which came to him suddenly like a gust of wind, and yet he was certain that he had to act now before Bob and his mother finished their work and noticed that he was missing. The plan was simple. He would run to the beach, watch the dolphins sail across the horizon, and then run back to the house. At most, he would be gone only for a few minutes, since the ocean was close, so close.

Nothing at that moment was more alluring than the sound of the water just beyond the dunes.

V

The early afternoon air began to feel noticeably warmer, and for a few seconds it was difficult to breathe, as if he were under water and couldn't inhale enough air to satisfy his thirsty lungs. He didn't panic, however, because he realized that he was in a strange environment and that there were things swirling all around him that were difficult and upsetting. He was slightly uncomfortable with his decision, although neither this discomfort nor his labored breathing was enough to make him wait for Bob and his mother to take him to the beach. In fact, as soon as the air began to cool and his breathing became normal and easy, he slipped quietly around the house to the back yard, where there was a large open field of dirt and weeds that stretched from the edge of the patio to the bottom of the dunes. With his back against the house, and out of sight of the large windows overhead, he breathed deeply several times to steady himself and then pushed off from the house and walked toward the dunes, in full view of anyone looking out the windows. Since there was no way of reaching the dunes without exposing himself to the windows, he stopped some twenty yards from the house, looked over his left shoulder to see if someone was watching him, and, when he was confident that he hadn't been observed, began running toward the dunes as fast as he could, dodging weeds, jumping over small holes, and kicking aside the occasional can or bottle until he reached the bottom of a towering mountain of sand.

The dune looked different up close than it did from the porch. It was much larger than he had imagined and, instead of glistening like a mountain of pink jewels, the sand looked dull, brown, and dirty. There were also small, grayish weeds everywhere, which, once they were uprooted, rolled limply down the dune to the bottom next to his shoes. Timmy might have backed away from this uninspiring mass of sand and dirt, except that there was no other way of reaching the dolphins on the other side than by scaling the dune. Still, he hesitated before taking another step. Despite his determination to continue on regardless of what Bob and his mother said, he needed to hear the waves to make sure that they were encouraging him to see the dolphins while he still had a chance, before they moved on to another part of the world. Surprisingly, the boom and hiss were fainter here than at the house, and when a slight gust of wind blew off the top of the dunes, sprinkling sand down to the very bottom, he could hardly hear anything at all. But what he could hear seemed as familiar to him as his own bedroom, with all his toys and the giant dolphin book, and he couldn't help thinking that the barely perceptible hiss was calling his name – a name that seemed peculiar and unfamiliar but was just as personal and defining – and inviting him to the water's edge before it was too late. Timmy turned around to take one last look at the house and its windows. Even now, he might have stopped had Bob and his mother been in sight, but it was clear that they had other things on their minds, and so he turned and began trudging up the dune.

Climbing the dune was not a simple task. Timmy had thought that he could run up the dune as easily as he had run across the field, bouncing over weeds and sidestepping holes and other obstructions. But he didn't realize that unlike the dirt field, the surface of the dune was soft, and each time he stepped onto the dune, his feet sank below the surface, preventing quick moves and filling his shoes with sand. Not only that, he was having trouble keeping his balance. Initially, he tried to walk up the dune, but the inclination and looseness of the sand quickly forced him onto his hands and feet. Even then he slipped several times and once, about a quarter of the way up the dune, he suddenly lost his balance and began sliding down toward the bottom. Somehow, he managed to catch hold of a particularly tenacious weed with a long stem topped by a yellow flower and, grasping it with all his might, he was able to stop his downward trajectory, straighten himself, and then continue back up the dune, this time with greater care than before. Forty minutes later, he finally reached the summit, and he was so tired that he could barely pull himself up and onto the flat ridge, where he collapsed, his eyes closed and his body motionless, facing the ocean.

The air was cool, almost cold, which seemed to intensify the peculiar smell of the water. The smell, however, was pleasant, reminding him of the smell of the water inside the aquarium, which increased his conviction that there were dolphins in the water, probably only a few feet from where the water washed onto the sand.

Slowly opening his eyes, Timmy turned away from the water and, instead, looked down the face of the dune to where it flowed into the beach. He had expected this side of the dune to be a mirror image of the other side, but surprisingly it was only half as high and sloped so gently toward the beach that he was certain that he could walk to the water without much of an effort. But while he quickly regained his strength, and was increasingly confident that he could reach the beach in less than a minute, he still hesitated and remained motionless, preferring for the time being to survey the side of the dune and admire the manner in which at its base it became indistinguishable from the beach.

Timmy, despite his determination to see the dolphins, was reluctant to take the next step, either to continue on with his plan or to return and wait for his mom and Bob. It had been relatively easy to get this far (absent the difficulties climbing the dune), but to take a step in either direction now would take greater a determination and a willingness to accept the consequences – on the one hand, going back meant never seeing the dolphins, but on the other, going forward meant punishment and probably never again seeing the beach. While he struggled to weigh each side of the equation, he couldn't help wondering what his Grandpa would do in his shoes. Of course, he would have done as he pleased, but what would the old man have advised him to do? Timmy was certain that had he still been alive, he would have taken him to see the dolphins and "that, my lovely young boy, is that," he would have told his mother. But that wasn't enough. Timmy needed to know what Grandpa would say now, as if he were sitting next to him, holding and stroking his hand, explaining to him how life works. Tears filled his eyes at the thought of his Grandpa, and a sudden gust of wind suddenly swept across the dune, chilling his sweat-moistened tee-shirt and forcing him to shield his face from the sand that was pushing into his nose and eyes. By the time the wind died down, Timmy had made his decision, one which was reinforced by the sight that unfolded before him as he opened his eyes and beheld, for the very first time, the glistening, silver world that he had only seen in his dreams.

The light reflecting off the steel-blue water was intense, and instinctively he shielded his eyes with both hands. He couldn't close his eyes, though, or even turn away from a world that seemed to stretch for eternity, a world that had been drawing him toward it all his life, a world that strangely seemed more like home than anything he left behind. Convinced that he could find the dolphins, Timmy rolled over the top of the dune and tumbled down all the way until the slope met the beach and leveled off, leaving him only feet from the water – and the dolphins.

VI

Timmy was covered with fine, white sand. He could see it on his clothes. He could feel it on his skin and in his hair. When he bent over to look at his feet, he could feel tiny rills of sand running off his head and then see the sand leap off his body and fall onto the beach, where it disappeared among all the other countless grains spread across the beach. It was a pleasant feeling, and for a couple of seconds he imagined himself to be an hourglass, counting off the time by the smallest degree possible.

Determined not to lose any more time, Timmy jumped up and ran across the sand to the edge of the water, where he met the remnants of a large wave that was sweeping across the beach. The cold, hissing water rushed over his feet and then swelled almost to his knees, soaking his pants and making him shiver. Even though he was freezing, he was thrilled by the experience and surprised by the strange texture of the water – it felt thicker and heavier than the water at home – and by its wondrously briny smell. Timmy had seen any number of pictures of the ocean, and he had also seen a few movies with beaches in them just like this one, but none of these things gave him any sense of what he was finally experiencing for himself. Looking down at the water surrounding his legs, he marveled at the sparkling streams that wound their way around his legs and then receded along the same path back to the ocean, digging the sand out from beneath his feet and pulling him toward the ocean. It was hard not to believe that the ocean was calling him – his name echoing in the roar and hiss of the water -- at the behest of the dolphins, who were out in the depths somewhere waiting for the chance to reveal themselves to him.

Timmy quickly scanned the horizon for dolphins, but all he saw was an endless stretch of blue punctuated here and there by troops of pelicans, occasionally dipping their lower jaws into the water to pick up fish before returning to their orderly progression. He wasn't disappointed, though. His mom and Bob might have used the absence of dolphins as proof that waters on this stretch of the coast were barren of the animals, but he knew they would come; he knew that they would arise out of the water sooner or later and that he would be there to see them. He couldn't have made it this far if nothing was out there waiting for him. Once again, Timmy felt the cold water wash across his feet and surround his ankles.

Looking down at the small currents of sparkling sunlight that tickled his toes as they slipped back into the ocean, Timmy couldn't help thinking that he had never seen water as beautiful as this before; not even the dark blue lakes or the crystalline streams that filled some of his mom's magazines could compare to what he was now seeing for the first time. And yet it wasn't the water that impressed him so much as the idea that he was finally standing in water that might have washed off a dolphin's back as it rose out of the water and reached for the clouds, its long, smiling snout pointing toward the sun, or engulfed the dolphin as it slipped back under the surface in search of food or fun.

Timmy got down on his knees and then sat back on his heels, as another wave swept around him. From this position, the water rose to his shoulders and droplets of water finer than grains of sand sprayed his face before, once again, flowing back away from him. The water may still have been cold, but he was no longer freezing – he felt warm and comfortable, as if the water was as natural to him as the sand under his knees – and even after it receded and he was left kneeling in his wet clothes, the wind shaking his shirt and pants, he felt as warm and comfortable as he did when he took long, warm baths each evening before school. But there was more to this sensation than warmth – when the water surrounded him, he was ready to believe that it was embracing him, comforting him, and sounds from the waves were instructing him to be impatient because they were on their way. This sensation was so strong that rather than release it or let it go, he tried to hold onto it by closing his eyes and reliving it, imagining that this was the very same feeling that dolphins experience as they glide through the water.

With his eyes still closed, Timmy leaned back on his hands and turned his face toward the sun. The warmth of the sun on his face, shoulders, and chest, added to the pleasant feeling as the water continued to flow and ebb around his body, gently rocking him as if he were still a baby in his mom's or Grandpa's arms. Once, however, the water receded rapidly and, instead of rocking, he felt as if he were rising out of the sea like a dolphin breaching the surface of the water and sensing the warm sun on its tender skin, after which, as the water returned, he could feel himself slipping beneath the surface, diving down to the bottom where he could swim with the other dolphins. But just as the water seemed to stop and swirl around his neck and chin, he had a strange sensation that he was not alone, that there were others nearby, and that these others were dolphins. Timmy opened his eyes expecting to see dolphins, and instead he was hit in the face by a large wave.

The wave was violent and aggressive, and it not only knocked him backwards but also forced him under the surface, where he was surrounded by a mist of roiling bubbles and sea foam. Once under the surface, Timmy could feel himself being forced head over heels by the action of the wave, and there was nothing he could do to stabilize himself no matter how he flailed his arms and legs. Water filled his nose and lungs and his eyes burned, and he needed air desperately. But just as quickly as the wave arose from the sea, it subsided, leaving Timmy flat on his stomach facing the receding water.

Coughing and gasping for breath, Timmy's entire body ached and his eyes and nose burned unbearably. It took perhaps five minutes for Timmy's coughing to subside, and shortly after that he began to sneeze, and he sneezed perhaps forty times in a row before that, too, subsided. Eventually, Timmy was able to breath normally, although his chest ached whenever he inhaled a little too heavily, and his eyes hurt and the inside of his nose felt raw, as if something had gone into his nose and scraped the area between his eyes.

Timmy pushed himself back from the water. Only when he was far enough away from the tip of the waves did he feel safe enough to lie down, cradle his head in his arms, and close his eyes. The sand was soft and warm, and as the sun's heat came to rest on his back and shoulders, he felt as comfortable as he had ever felt in bed, especially because his senses were infused with the soothing sounds of the waves, the smells of the water and sand, and the clatter of the occasional gull. Timmy luxuriated in the darkness now surrounding him. It was wonderful to feel and hear everything surrounding him and yet not be able to see a single thing, which for a while made him feel as though he were floating in some strange, magical world in which only an occasional falling star and the spectral images of frolicking dolphins could be seen and felt. One of these dolphins, a large, smiling male that was surrounded by a bright sky and shimmering ocean, had come so close that Timmy couldn't resist reaching out and trying to touch its bony snout; but the very instant that his fingers came within a hair's breath of the animal, it vanished in the darkness and was replaced by the smiling face of his Grandpa, who briefly nodded in affirmation before he, too, vanished into the dark nothingness. Suddenly, Timmy's ability to float endlessly ceased, and he began to fall, slowly tumbling head over heels as if he were once again under the waves. Timmy gripped the sand with his fingers and toes to arrest the movement, but when even that failed to halt his downward spiral, he opened his eyes as wide as he could. For a few seconds, the light from the sun was blinding, but as he dipped his head to temper the brightness he could see the light of the sun reflecting off the water, which approached but did not quite reach him. Even though the sensation of tumbling stopped, he immediately vomited a couple of times.

Timmy felt better, although it took several minutes before the acrid taste left his mouth; and as he watched the remnants of his breakfast expand in the watery sand and then gradually make their way to the ocean, he wondered what might have happened had he not been able to force his way out of the wave. After all, he couldn't swim.

VII

Timmy's Grandpa had visited two summers ago, arriving with three bulging suitcases filled with clothes, books on ocean life, and a dozen or so small figurines of sea animals. Timmy's mother wasn't pleased with the advent of more toys, because, she claimed, Timmy had enough trouble taking care of the toys he had. Nevertheless, she relented and allowed the toys to stay, particularly because the figurines were rather interesting and surprisingly realistic. Among the figurines were a salmon, a sawfish, a swordfish, a hammerhead shark, a stingray, an octopus, an eel, a crab, a lobster, a number of indeterminate fish, and a dolphin. The dolphin, whose gray, sleek body had a strange rubbery texture, was larger and even more realistic than the other figurines (the whites of its eyes were visible, and it was possible to feel the natural striations in its skin by running one's index finger on the underside of its body), and ever since then dolphins had been the central, guiding passion of Timmy's life.

Timmy would never forget the trip because his Grandpa never tired of answering questions about the figurines, sea life, and especially the dolphin and its real-life brothers and sisters. He could still remember asking him questions about the size of dolphins, their colors, the texture of their skin, where they lived, how they lived, what they ate, if fish bones ever got stuck in their throats, what they did during the night, if they had enemies, if they liked people, if they would like him, and if he could touch one. When he wasn't answering questions, his Grandpa would play with him, both of them pretending to be great dolphins out in the middle of the ocean, leaping high into the air and then diving deep under the dark water. Usually, Timmy was the dolphin that would leap into the air, because his Grandpa was slightly unsteady on his feet, and so he would often dive as deep as he could bend his "old knees." Timmy sometimes had the impression that his mom and Bob weren't too keen on the games his Grandpa played with him or the books and toys he brought for his "education," as he liked to say with a big smile, because one or the other would often grumble about what Grandpa did or said; and one time, over the dinner table, when Grandpa explained to Timmy about the nobility of the great mammals in the ocean, Bob objected and said that there was nothing noble about ocean life and that the animals in it were meant to be eaten.

"Would you eat a dolphin?" Grandpa asked, glowering at him.

"Put it on my plate and you'll see," he retorted and then left the table.

None of this deterred his Grandpa. Timmy's Grandpa wasn't the type of person to be deterred. And Timmy remembered the conversation, because later that evening in his bedroom the old man told him about the beauty of ocean life and explained how dolphins, above all creatures on the earth, were noble and lived lives that we could only dream about. He contrasted dolphin life with the ignobility and violence of human life.

"You see," he said, lowering his voice so that Bob couldn't hear them talking, "You see, the whales and dolphins live peacefully with one another, unlike human beings, and they help one another in ways that people, even family members, are sometimes reluctant to do." Timmy couldn't completely understand what the old man was saying, but he was impressed by the way he was saying it and, of course, he loved his Grandpa.

"I have always wondered if I was part dolphin myself. Not because I can swim particularly well. I like to help people, I like to help those I love, especially you, my dearest little Timmy." The old man picked up the dolphin figurine and asked him to imagine a small dolphin baby swimming by its side (using his left hand to represent the dolphin baby, he held the figurine and showed him how they might swim through the water, leaping, diving, and breathing). "Look at this, Sweetie, do you see how the mother dolphin is caring for its baby, keeping it close to her side so that it can nurse and breathe when needed? She will never let the baby leave her side until it is old and mature enough to live on its own. And after this, it will take care of its elders in the same way that the mother cared for it."

27

"Do you mean....?"

"No, of course not," he continued, knowing full well the mind of a boy Timmy's age and the limits of such a boy's understanding. "No, when her baby is grown, he will protect his elders so that they can grow gracefully into old age and nothing bad ever happens to them."

"Like what?"

"Well, there are all kinds of dangers in the ocean. There are dangerous fish like sharks, but even more dangerous are people, who don't care what happens to ocean life – and that means killing the animals and leaving the human stuff (you know, hooks, nets, beer cans) lying around so animals get trapped and hurt and killed. The baby, when it's old enough, does his best to protect its family, or whoever it's closest to, from these things; and as soon as it has children, it teaches the children to treasure life and show respect to its elders. Do you know something else?" he asked and turned to the right and then the left to make sure that no one but Timmy heard what he was going to say. "Do you know something else? Dolphins live in one big, happy family, where everyone takes care of everyone else, and the elders are respected, not treated like a nuisance, like something you toss aside whenever you don't have any use for it. It's true."

His Grandpa leaned back and his rough, flabby cheeks shook slightly as he smiled at Timmy and patted him gently on the head.

Timmy quietly examined the figurine while his Grandpa sat next to him, watching him play and answering his questions about dolphins (most, if not all, of his questions concerned dolphins, even though he liked the other animals, too). Timmy noticed from time to time that his mom and Bob would look over at the two of them, but they apparently didn't care to engage in the conversations about dolphins or other sea animals.

Timmy stared at the waves crashing onto the beach as he thought about his Grandpa. The memory of his Grandpa should have been a pleasant one (perhaps tinged around the edges with sadness) because he was going to see dolphins this day, and there would have been nothing that the old man would have wanted Timmy to see and experience more than dolphins in the wild. Instead, the memory was, for a few moments at least, a heavy one, because Timmy realized that his Grandpa would never be there to see them and that he would never be able to tell his Grandpa about his experiences or about the beauty of the great mammals of the sea.

The last day was a sad day. Last days were always sad days, because he couldn't stand to see his Grandpa leave, even if he knew that he would soon return; but on this occasion, it was doubly sad because the old man was having a particularly difficult time leaving Timmy. Timmy would never forget that day. He could still see the back of his Grandpa -- his baggy gray coat partly tucked into the back of his pants (doubtless a mistake that the old man in his sorrow had not noticed) and his body listing heavily to the right because of the weight of the suitcase he was carrying – as he walked to the taxi. He walked very slowly, more slowly than normal, and even though the taxi was only a few feet from the door, he paused two or three times to catch his breath and sniff heavily. Running out the door and catching up with the old man, Timmy was taken aback by how profusely his Grandpa was sweating, which he wiped off his face with a yellowish handkerchief that he pulled from his coat when he stopped as Timmy came up to him. Grandpa gave him a brisk, one-armed hug, after which he watched as the old man struggled into the taxi, straining himself to get comfortable and then tucking his coat out of the way so that it wouldn't get trapped in the door. After he had settled in and, once again, wiped the sweat from his face, he pulled Timmy close to him and whispered in his ear that he loved him more than anything else in the world and promised never to leave him for long. Timmy had always regretted not saying anything in response, because no one meant more to him than his Grandpa and because he counted on the old man to keep his promise.

His Grandpa only visited one more time, which ended up being the time he had taken Timmy to the aquarium. It was on that occasion, too, that the old man expressed his love for the boy, although more tearfully, and Timmy clearly remembered the man again saying that he would be with him forever. The old man also noted that while a few people are close to dolphins ("You and me, for example," he noted), his mom and Bob were not among them.

VIII

Something inside Timmy warned him that he should be farther back from the water. But the lure of dolphins was too great and, besides, with his strength back and senses clear, there was very little that the ocean had left to show him and so, with a little caution, he could safely remain where he was or even move an inch or two closer to the water to get a better view of the dolphins when they came. Instead of standing up and facing the sea, however, Timmy pivoted on his belly until, once again, he faced the slate-blue water and could look out over the increasingly hazy horizon.

Unfortunately, there wasn't much to see at this point, other than an endless stretch of water broken every now and then by the white crest of a wave and, of course, the occasional gray silhouette of the pelicans as they glided farther out to sea. He was worried, though, that the chance of seeing the dolphins was diminishing, because a gray haze was slowly settling on the water, obscuring the distant waves and absorbing the pelicans farthest from the shore. Timmy wasn't ready to give up. He knew they were there, and he knew he could find them before his time ran out, and so he scanned the waters even more intently, watching each successive wave as it inched closer, racing up the beach and practically kissing his chin, for any telltale signs of dolphins.

And he didn't retreat when the waves did touch his chin, because they reminded him of the times when his Grandpa would grab him gently on the chin and tell him that he loved him or that he was proud of him. Of course, Timmy was coming to an age when such overt displays of affection – particularly in public – were slightly embarrassing, and yet it was the memory of these displays of his Grandpa's love that would never cease to comfort him and would stay with him throughout his final minutes and seconds. Naturally, his mom and Bob would have laughed at Timmy's assertion that the ocean reminded him of his Grandpa, since the ocean could not express love or be loved like a human being – "It's only water," his mom would have said, and she would have railed against his Grandpa's affections and his "constant efforts to fill your head with nonsense" – but there could be no denying that as the water wrapped itself around his arms and legs, it was embracing him, making him feel wanted just like his Grandpa made him feel wanted, as if his spirit somehow inhabited the sweet-tasting ocean.

Timmy continued to scan the waters for the dolphins that were sure to reveal themselves any moment. Every now and then a larger, faster wave than expected would sweep across the beach and crash into his face, forcing warm water into his eyes and mouth, but none of this fazed him or made him think any less of the water, or even brought back the unfortunate incident that sent him tumbling in the foamy water only moments ago. Each time the water overstepped its bounds, Timmy would simply wipe his face and eyes with the back of his hand, spit out any sand that managed to work its way into his mouth, and resume his search for the near mythical animals.

One wave, however, was so strong that it knocked Timmy's head backward and sent him sliding leftward along the beach. He recovered quickly this time, because his eyes had been closed when the water struck and he had been able to hold his breath before the water actually entered his mouth. He was also extremely lucky, for when he opened his eyes and was instantly able to see clearly, he noticed some short, dark streaks along the horizon, or just in front of the wall of haze that continued coming his way. Unfortunately, they were too far away to identify immediately, but there was something about them that attracted his attention, something about the way they moved in and out of the water – like a large, moving wheel, one would arc out of the water while another would arc back into the water, and the movement would be repeated over and over – that made him wonder of he was finally coming face to face with the very things he had dreamed of seeing – dolphins.

Timmy watched the streaks for some time. For most of this time, they seemed content to skirt the horizon, staying away from the wall of mist that was inching its way toward the shore. But just as the mist was about to push them within a few hundred yards of the shore, they suddenly changed direction and moved off to the far right, where the mist appeared to be evaporating. There they hovered, seemingly forever, while Timmy strained his eyes to make out their shapes, to determine whether or not he was actually seeing what he hoped he was seeing.

It was clear that the movements of the streaks were not random. In fact, there was something almost choreographed about the way they moved in and out of the water, always in pairs and always with the same movements, as if the streaks were nothing but shadows of some invisible machine churning its way across the water. However, it was clear from the little nuances in their movements that these weren't machines of any sort but animals, either dolphins or large fish of some kind. Timmy obviously hoped they were dolphins, but he needed to make sure. He didn't want to tell anyone that he had seen dolphins only to find out that there was another explanation for the shapes, an explanation that would make people like his mother laugh at his folly. Timmy needed to be sure, and he wasn't going to leave until he was, even if the water continued to sweep him across the beach.

Luckily, he didn't have to wait that long. Just as the haze appeared to engulf the streaks like it was doing to every thing else across the water, the fish suddenly emerged right in front of him, not more than twenty or thirty feet from the shore.

IX

It was astounding. The fish were so close that he could practically touch them, so close that their proximity filled him with the desire to go into the water, to follow them as they broke the surface of the shimmering water and then, arching downward, disappeared only to resurface at some other nearby location. More than anything else at that moment, he wanted to touch their silky bodies, to caress the large fins that followed them in and out of the water, and to play with them. Their movements, the easy manner in which they glided in and out of the water, rolled from one side to another, poked their heard out of the water, clearly showed that they were playing, even if he couldn't understand the rules of the game. Timmy wanted to join in their fun. He, too, wanted to jump in and out of the water, roll from side to side, and do everything else they were doing.

But the more he watched these strange fish frolic in the warm, misty air – and the closer they inched toward him and the shore – the greater his doubts became as to whether these were indeed fish or some other animal. "I've never seen fish jump out of the water like that," he reminded himself, "and fish don't have smooth bodies or large fins in the center of their backs." While he continued to ponder over these strange creatures, one of them suddenly flew out of the water to his left and dove back into it with a splash that was loud enough for him to hear. Unfortunately, this happened too quickly for him to get a good view of the animal, but what he had seen added to his doubts that these animals were mere fish. Of course, "sharks have smooth skin and fins on their backs," he corrected himself, "but can they jump out of the water like that one just did?"

Unconsciously, Timmy began to inch closer and closer to the water and to the fish, or whatever they were. He could feel the water engulf him and his body bounce with each successive wave. It didn't matter. In fact, it felt good, and it made him feel emotionally closer to the creatures, almost close enough to engage in the play. "But what are these things?" he asked himself out loud, the water now up to his neck. But no sooner had he uttered his question than one of the animals leaped out of the water not more than ten feet from him. Unlike all his other sightings, this one was crystal clear – he saw the animal from nose to tail and in a strange silver light that functioned almost like a spotlight, and he knew that it was the very animal that he had come to see.

Even though Timmy had never seen a dolphin outside of the aquarium, but there was no confusing what he was now witnessing with anything else. Besides, he had seen enough dolphins in the aquarium and in his book to know the difference between a real dolphin and a shark or any other fish. And there was no mistaking the fact that the dolphins were coming closer and closer to the water's edge and that he could now see quite clearly their distinctive snouts and the beautiful smiles that graced their faces – smiles that matched the ebullience of their swimming and acrobatics, smiles that reflected the joy that they experienced every day as they swam the deep blue seas.

Timmy craned his head above the water as the dolphins moved closer and closer to the shore. There were ten, perhaps fifteen, of them, but he couldn't be sure because the water was bubbling up around his eyes and because they were moving so fast. Two or three or more at a time flew past him, slapping their tails in his direction as if they were calling out to him. He could hear their distinctive clicks and squeals, but the movement of their tails and the manner in which they slapped the water made him feel that they were trying to convey something very important to him. But what was it? What were they trying to say?

Every now and then the water rushed over his face, momentarily filling his nose with sea foam, but it hardly mattered any more, not with the dolphins so close and so obviously desirous of communicating with him; and, besides, he was finding that it was easy to blow the foam out of his nose without feeling a thing during or after. Indeed, blowing water and foam out his nose was beginning to seem as natural as breathing, and after a bit he began to do it unconsciously, as if he had done it all his life. But as he struggled to understand what the dolphins were saying to him, their clicks slowly became less distinct and more constant and melodious. He wasn't completely aware of the transition, but it was increasingly clear to him was that he was listening to music, beautiful music, emanating from dolphins and not simply crude clicks coming from dumb beasts, as his mother would have called them.

The music, which sounded like human voices softly singing, seemed to surround him, engulfing him in melodies that he had never heard before, and as he struggled to identify the specific dolphins who were singing to him (at one time, it sounded as if only a couple of dolphins were singing to him, while at another he would have sworn that hundreds if not thousands of these lovely voices were harmonizing from every direction imaginable), he noticed that several of the dolphins had come very close to him, some practically eye to eye, and at one point two, maybe three dolphins had come so close that they brushed up against him, gently as if they were petting him. Initially, he was surprised, but his surprise quickly melted and as it did, more and more dolphins surrounded him, petting him, singing to him, reaching out to him as if he were one of them, not merely a human being.

Timmy couldn't have explained it, he didn't have the words to describe his feelings, but at that very instant he knew that he had come to the water's edge for something very important. He was certain, without knowing why, that he had been led there by forces more powerful than any he had ever experienced living in his small, circumscribed world. Realistically, how could he have resisted? He was too small and lacked the strength to resist, and hadn't his mother always told him that he wasn't big enough to make up his own mind? But it didn't matter – he was finally face to face with something that he had dreamed about, something that he had wanted all his young life.

Suddenly, Timmy began to feel strange. At first, this sensation was little more than a slight dizziness, which might have been expected due to his tumbling earlier, but unlike that feeling this didn't relent, and after a while his dizziness grew more intense and the nausea that he had felt after tumbling came back, forcing him to retch several times. For a few seconds after this, everything seemed to be fine – the dizziness faded and the sick feeling began to subside and, for a moment or two, it appeared to have vanished entirely. Timmy had been able to shake off the last remnants of the feeling with a flick of his head, as if he were flicking the hair off his forehead, but then something else slammed into him, tearing away every ounce of control that he might have still had over his body. The pain was unlike anything he had ever felt before. When he was younger, he had once fallen off the front steps, banging his head, scraping his knees, and injuring his right arm. These injuries caused him much suffering, but nothing like the burning sensation he was experiencing now – it felt like a rush of flame had hit him and engulfed his entire body, searing off his skin and melting his bones. He tried to brush the flame off and run from the water, but he was too weak, or the force arrayed against him was too strong, and he could feel himself being pulled inexorably toward a caldron of molten fire and scalding steam. There was, however, a brief moment during which both the pain and the inexorable pull toward the water seemed to be ebbing – his skin was almost numb, and he could move his legs in small, inch-like steps toward the shore – but this was clearly an illusion, because something grabbed him on his head and feet and began stretching his body, pulling him to the point at which he was certain he would be ripped in two.

Timmy wanted to scream, he wanted to beg his Grandpa to reach down from heaven and pull him out of this fiery caldron, but he couldn't move his mouth properly to form anything other than screeches and peculiar clicking sounds that emanated from deep within his throat (he feared that his tongue and lips had been seared away by the superheated water). He wanted to cry, but he was unable to accomplish even this, as the only water flowing over his eyes was salty sea water, which was now rushing into his mouth and nose, choking him until everything started to become dark and silent.

The pain immediately disappeared, and the only thing he felt in its wake was an overwhelming desire for air.

X

Something was hitting him in the stomach. The blows were hard and blunt, as if someone was hitting him with a broom handle, and the force was such that with each successive blow, he could feel himself moving upward, slowly and steadily, toward the hazy blue light. He would have done almost anything to flee the discomfort, which seemed to be increasing with each successive blow, but he was too weak physically and too tired mentally to do anything except submit.

The blows abruptly stopped, however, when his head burst through the haze and he came face to face with the smooth surface of the slate-blue water. The water stretched endlessly in every direction, and because low, fuzzy clouds were resting on the surface near the horizon, it was difficult to tell where the water ended and the sky began. He was suddenly poked again, this time with a force that lifted his body out of the water and practically turned his lungs inside out, making him inhale a deep gulp of warm, sweet air. Surprisingly, the air eased the pain in his stomach and satisfied him in a way that no meal or tasty treat could have done.

He felt better after the air, and he could feel his strength and mental alertness returning. He looked around at the clouds in the sky and then at the horizon, as if he was seeing them for the first time, or as if he was seeing them after a long absence; and then he turned and stared down into the abyss below him. It seemed to be blank and featureless, and yet something inside told him that there was something down there, something that he needed to see. He hesitated, not knowing what to do or even what to think, and then with a movement that was as natural as it was instinctive, he arched his back and slipped beneath the surface of the water.

Closing his eyes, he began drifting downward, slowly at first, as if he were sliding head first down the edge of a soft cloud, but within a few minutes he began to move faster, and the soft cloud disappeared and he felt as though he were falling from a high building, his speed increasing with every inch he moved. Sensing that he had gone far enough, maybe too far, he arched his stomach, stretching his muscles with all his strength, until he had come to a complete stop, no longer nose down but seemingly parallel with the surface. He didn't move for some time – he didn't know what to do next – but sensing that he was again beginning to move downward (albeit very slowly, almost imperceptivity), he moved his nose upward slightly and his lower body downward slightly and, to his surprise, he started to move forward, not very quickly, but at least he no longer had the sensation of falling. His forward momentum didn't last very long, and once again he had the sensation of floating slowly downward. Repeating the movement stopped his descent and propelled him forward, and another repetition of the movement pushed him forward again, only a little faster and a little farther. He repeated it over and over, moving his entire body up and down, moving as if his arms and legs were tied to his body, or as if he no longer needed arms and legs to swim quickly and efficiently. He continued pushing his body up and down, gliding through the water like a paper airplane moving on a gust of air, and as he did so he could feel himself gaining strength and agility by the second, despite the fact that he wasn't breathing and didn't seem to need air. With his eyes still closed, he began to dream about flying, about floating in an endless night sky where neither cloud nor wind slowed his forward motion, and for a few moments he couldn't help wondering why there was no moon or stars in the sky, despite the ease with which he seemed to able to leave the earth's pull and soar freely throughout space. He had seen space from the earth, but he had never imagined how wonderful it could be to float through space, moving freely, effortlessly, without anything to hinder his movements. He stopped moving just to soak up the sensation.

Once again, he was hit in the stomach with the broom handle, but this time he immediately opened his eyes, turned, and angling himself upward, began swimming toward the surface using only the lower portion of his body. The hazy, indistinct light overhead returned and as soon as he reached the shimmering surface of the water, it shattered into millions of tiny iridescent bubbles that quickly coalesced around him on the now-familiar flat, endless plain that merged seamlessly in all directions with the sky. He paused here, too, and, looking around he saw the same ocean, the same clouds, and same endlessness as before, but this time something was different – and this different something resided not in the surrounding seascape but in himself, even though he didn't understand it or couldn't understand it at this point in his life. While he was looking around, trying to understand what had changed, he noticed several strange sounds seemingly emanating from behind him but echoing all around him; it was clear from the crispness and clarity of the sounds that they didn't emanate from under the water, and yet there were no signs anywhere of the origin of the sounds. "Puff, puff, puff" went the sounds, slowly and periodically, not all at once, and each time he heard a 'puff' he felt better, stronger, as if these strange sounds were nourishing his body in a way that he hadn't realized until now that it needed. He was about to leave and put the sounds behind him (which to some extent they were) when he realized that the sounds coincided with his own efforts to clear his lungs and breathe. He had never heard anything like that from himself – and he couldn't understand why his breathing should sound so dramatically different than it had throughout all the years he had been breathing – but the fact that he was breathing and that he didn't in the least feel ill (the sporadic breaths made him fell better than he had in some time) satisfied his curiosity and eased every concern that he had had at the moment. With one last 'puff,' he again pointed his nose toward the water, arched his back, and slipped easily beneath the surface of the water and, with a flick of the lower portion of his body, sailed downward into the depths.

He wasn't going to go as deep this time, however. Something inside him told him that the water was much shallower now and that he needed to exercise extreme caution the deeper he went. And, unlike last time, he kept his eyes open, even though for a few minutes there wasn't much to see. The water all around him was empty and suffused with a bluish glow from above, but as he got deeper the water became darker and grayer until he couldn't see anything. He could easily have been persuaded that his eyes were closed, except that he was positive that they were open and had been open from the very second he reentered the water. Leveling off and slowing down, he hesitated and opened and closed his eyes several times to make sure that his eyes were indeed open and, once they started becoming acclimated to the dim light, squinting and rolling them to clear his vision. He wasn't nervous, and he didn't feel apprehensive about being so far beneath the surface, where it could take as long as a minute or more to reach the surface for a breath of air. On the contrary, he felt comfortable, despite his cloudy vision, as if being under the water was as natural as being almost anywhere else. Once his eyes adjusted to the darkness, he looked around just as he had looked around when poking his head out of the water.

The hazy, blue surface of the water hovered above him as before, although off to his right it was punctuated by the yellowish, circular glow of what appeared to be the sun. A dense, featureless wall of blue water surrounded him and prevented him from seeing more than a few hundred feet in either direction. Staring straight ahead and looking for signs of life, he noticed tiny, almost imperceptible, glittering flakes of something surrounding him and then, as he looked beyond the flakes, small streams of bubbles occasionally floating upward until they disappeared somewhere near the surface. For a while, everything was deadly still except for an occasional shriek coming from somewhere in the distance beyond his sight, but as he listened and tried to make sense of this strange world, he noticed some odd clicking sounds, faint at first but increasing in volume, and then the sounds of bubbles, croaks, groans, clicks, swishes, and an array of other noises that he couldn't identify. Most of these seemed to be rising from below him, and as he leaned downward, his nose pointing straight down, he noticed a nearly endless expanse of rocks, sand, and small, encrusted tubes protruding out of the sand and spitting out fine particles of something that rose a few feet and then settled down on the strange deformations and convolutions he intuitively recognized as coral.

He was amazed. Each glob, deformation, encrustation, or tube was now suffused with bright, glowing colors – deep reds, intense yellows, pale greens, and every variety in between – and here and there wavy sea grasses lazily moved back and forth in response to the current and the strange fish that moved in and out of the grasses, feeding and seeking shelter. There were fish everywhere and in every shape and size imaginable -- long silver ones, red and yellow striped ones, tiny ones, huge lumbering ones, flat

41

ones, ones with eyes on their sides and ones with eyes on their back, and a couple that he couldn't tell if they were fish, coral, or something else. One of these fish had an array of long spines protruding from every part of its body. Another, slender and rather dull orange, unexpectedly inflated like a balloon, and across its entire body were little spines like those of a porcupine. And if these things weren't surprising enough, he noticed a large, grayish ball that appeared to disappear and reappear every few minutes. As it floated closer to him, it became clear that it wasn't a ball but a school of small fish that pressed together whenever a large animal was nearby and quickly dispersed after the animal was out of sight. He shook his body twice just to see the fish swarm.

He couldn't take his eyes off the wonderful world spread out before him. But while he was taking in everything, including the nearly invisible movements of the ocean's currents (which could be determined not only by the swaying sea grasses but also by the movement of the glittering flakes and the settling of particles from the sea tubes), he caught sight of a long, slender shadow that floated across the coral before heading out and disappearing into the darkness beyond the reefs. The shadow didn't initially trouble him – it was more of a curiosity than anything else – but he did notice that while it lingered all of the bright, vibrant life on the seabed suddenly disappeared, giving everything a dull, almost deathlike appearance. Once the shadow was gone, however, everything reappeared as before – bright, colorful, and lively – and had he not seen it for himself, he would have sworn that there had never been a shadow or anything else hovering over this world. Curiously, it hadn't occurred to him to identify the source of the shadow and make sense of the strange reaction it elicited from the creatures and everything else here. He was too enthralled by everything, even the sinister changes caused by the presence of the shadow, to imagine that there could be anything untoward in this world, anything that he himself should fear. And yet shortly after it was gone, apparently for good, and life was back to normal, a shiver ran down his back and he could feel his heart race, but before he could understand this reaction another strong jab in the stomach immediately forced him upward. Shattering the surface, he greedily puffed air before quickly returning to the bustling world below.

Nothing prepared him for what he was now experiencing. It was unlike anything that he had ever imagined, despite having dreamed about it for as long as he could remember and having seen hundreds maybe thousands of pictures of the undersea world. Even his prized dolphin book offered only a pale representation of what now lay before him. It was extraordinary – what other word was there for what he was now seeing? -- and he felt as though some magical being had swept him up to the highest peak in the world and there spread out a mystical, miraculous world for his sole pleasure. But even more extraordinary than everything around him were the dolphins, which were now swimming on either side of him, accompanying him wherever he went.

Shortly after identifying the sleek, silver shapes of the dolphins surrounding him, he could feel himself picking up speed. The currents of the water began to rush past like the wind, and the sea floor was now a soft blur, as he flew past canyon after canyon, mountains of coral, and schools of sparking fish, which seemed to be desperate to move out of his way. It was strange to feel his body undulating like a long stick of rubber as he propelled himself along with the others, and yet nothing seemed more natural or more comfortable; and his body seemed to have a mind of its own, moving him where he needed to go so that he need do nothing except enjoy the ride and watch the undersea world spin by. Well, maybe this isn't entirely accurate. Every time he tried to move this way or that to make room for a dolphin or to avoid a fish or a large rock, he invariably bumped against a dolphin or two, often sending them into other dolphins. It was clear that he had a lot to learn, but surprisingly none of his little indiscretions met with anything more than a forgiving, playful smile.

XI

Those first few minutes, hours, days, and maybe even weeks were miraculous (he lost all sense of time, and so he couldn't tell how long he had been with the dolphins. Perhaps it had been a lifetime, although he still retained bits and pieces of his past life somewhere in his head). The world around him was strange and strangely inviting and he couldn't resist the temptation to explore everything he saw whether he recognized the thing (probably from one of his books) that attracted him or not. Luckily, the dolphins watched over him, and though they gave him the freedom to explore -- the coral, the seabed, the sea grasses, as well the animals and fishes, whether they swam through the waters, crawled across the sand, or hid themselves amid the rocks and corals – they were also careful to keep him away from some of the less obvious dangers lurking in the water. He was prohibited, for example, from swimming beyond the coral reefs unless the others accompanied him, because there was no safety in the dark, open water. Fortunately, he wasn't as interested in the dark, open water as much as he was fascinated by the bright, shallow water over the coral beds where the activities of the inhabitants rose to a fevered pitch toward the end of the day.

In fact, he was able to avoid many dangers on his own, using only his ability to maneuver quickly to avoid such monsters as eels, manta rays, and things that he had never seen before, not even in one of his books. This in itself was extraordinary. He couldn't explain how he had learned to swim so well, and yet from the very moment he opened his eyes in this new world, swimming came as naturally to him as eating and breathing. And he loved swimming more than anything else. He loved charging nose down in the clear water, pulling up just before he collided with the sea floor, and then shooting straight up toward the bright, shimmering light overhead until he shattered the surface with a loud swoosh. Floating through the crystalline morning air for a few seconds (it always seemed much longer), feeling the sun warming his back and the water rolling off his body, he would then slip quietly back into the water and once again head toward the bottom. He would often do this several times in a row or, when the mood suited him, he would hover just beneath the surface and, pushing up and down with the lower portion of his body, fly through the water as fast as he could go, as far as he could go, breaching only now and then to grab a lungful of air. There was no explanation for the impossibly quick acquisition of this skill, even though he had always believed that he would swim as well as a dolphin if given half a chance, and if the conditions in the water were right. Truly, the reason didn't matter; he was just happy that he could swim; he was also thrilled that the others stayed close to him most of the time, alternately swimming close to him and guiding his activities (that is, keeping him from being bored or getting into trouble), and spending time playing with him (most of the games at this point entailed avoiding one another as everyone swam together) and instructing him, as far as he could tell (since his facility with the language was limited, he was often hard to tell what they wanted him to do). Apart from these things, he was thrilled that over time he was able to keep up with the others as they moved from place to place, often for reasons that were completely obscure to him.

Well, he did his best to keep up with the others. It was often difficult, to say the least, to follow their movements and anticipate where they might go next. Sometimes, they would go from place to place, swimming side by side in unison as if their movements had all been choreographed and practiced over and over; at other times, they would charge back and forth, up and down, without rhyme or reason, as if they were all in a frightful panic, even if they weren't. He had studied their movements very carefully, and more than once was convinced that he had finally understood what precipitated their movements and motivated them to charge forward in an orderly fashion like a conquering army or to scatter pell-mell like a mass of retreating soldiers. But every time he felt the inward joy of finally solving a seemingly intractable problem, something invariably happened to upset all his calculations and he would end up metaphorically scratching his head and wondering, 'What are they doing, why are they doing that, and where are they going?' There was a time when he was convinced that food, play, security, and breathing dictated their directions and the manner in which they moved – that food, for instance, would drive them in one direction, play in another, security in another direction entirely, and air to the surface – but he quickly learned that what seemed to be inviolable laws governing their minds and movements was sooner or later violated by every member of the group (sometimes discarded entirely), leaving him bewildered and fearful that he was likely to make the wrong decision in any given situation. This is not to suggest that there weren't instances in which he had accurately anticipated their actions and had been able to move in lockstep with them like a shadow or mirror image. Indeed, there were, but such instances were rare and more often than not followed by others that left him frustrated and sometimes doubtful that he would ever get things right.

The only exception to this was breathing. They all seemed to need air at the same time, and so they would rise to the surface in a group, breach and breathe heavily more or less simultaneously, and then descend in more or less the same order, unless some or all of them decided to stay on the surface to play (which was always a possibility). Once he became accustomed to holding his breath and breathing at regular intervals, he was able to anticipate these movements with a high degree of accuracy, which sometimes made up for his inability to predict their other movements and gave him some hope of eventually understanding their behavior. The issue, of course, was that he never felt fully integrated into their society as long as he couldn't make heads or tails of their behavior. In retrospect, it was somewhat amusing to think that he had developed a rational understanding of their breathing behavior when it was simply a matter of lung capacity, and his was about the same as everyone else's. But at least this spared him some of the painful jabs that he had experience when he first joined them.

Indeed, his days of being "snouted," as he sometimes called it, for not breathing in unison with the others were soon gone, even though he was frequently snouted for other things such as not paying attention or going beyond the limits considered safe or comfortable by the others. As usual, he was rewarded for his indiscretion by a few well-placed bony snouts. But while these instructional corrections were painful, they didn't anger him or make him resentful, because, as he eventually realized, if it weren't for those who meted out punishment, he might have encountered some real

46

trouble -- dolphins who don't pay attention, dolphins who lag behind the others, or dolphins who become separated from the group rarely if ever survived in the wild. Dolphin society, as he quickly learned, was a communal society, and everything from finding food to protecting oneself depended on help and cooperation from the others. Later on, he would never forget the plight of one of the older dolphins who, lagging behind because of illness, disappeared in the dark waters, never to be heard from again. This alone was enough to make him appreciate (at times) the helpful nudges from the others, and it encouraged him to do everything he could to help the others to ensure his and their survival.

XII

More importantly, he had lots of friends among the dolphins. Everyone was friendly, everyone was willing to spend time with him either playing or teaching, and it didn't matter which because he loved them all in a way that he could never love people (with the single exception of his Grandpa). And it was obvious that they loved him. None of them could help smiling even if they just looked at him, which was something that he had never experienced as a human (once again, his Grandpa was the lone exception).

Nevertheless, there were times when the others treated him...well, differently than the others. Clearly, he was just the same as they were, albeit younger than most and inexperienced, but he sometimes had trouble understanding why, if they took so much trouble to protect, play, and instruct him, they sometimes acted as if he wasn't one of them, or as if he was one of them but not entitled to everything normally accorded to everyone else. It was hard to explain (most of this came as the result of his perceptions, not indisputable facts), but essentially he sometimes felt excluded from the activities in which the others often invested considerable time, making him feel that he was being forced to watch them from the outside, as if he were observing them through the long, circular window of the dolphin tank at the aquarium. This wasn't his completely his imagination. There were times, for example, when he was not allowed to approach the older females. Others were allowed, but when he approached, he was pushed off by a dozen or more bony snouts. It was more or less the same thing when he tried to join some of the strange games the males were playing at the same time. He was rebuffed, sometime stoutly, as if he was using these games to approach the females (this wasn't on his mind, although it was apparently on the mind of more than a few of the males). He eventually concluded that his rejections were related to his youth and inexperience, although something similar happened when he tried to approach the youngest dolphins, babies hardly more than a few days old. Others could approach them, nuzzle them toward the surface when necessary, and even play simple games with them, just as some of the older dolphins had played simple games with him once he had made his initial foray into the water. Despite his efforts brush these things off, they slowly added to his frustration over being unable to fully comprehend some of the dolphin ways, although he never felt that he was being treated as unfairly as he was treated as a human.

In fact, nothing the others did truly lowered them in his esteem, or dampened his joy in having transmuted from the human to the dolphin world. Nothing in their attitudes or behaviors made them seem more human and less like the dolphins that he had always dreamed about, if for no other reason than they were invariably friendly and smiling. This was significant. Unlike human beings, the dolphins always had a warm smile for him, which reflected their kind, loving, and attentive treatment of him. And it didn't matter what the situation was – feeding, playing, guarding – he could count on a loving smile from every dolphin even when he didn't deserve it. These smiles were not only reassuring (especially when he was lonely), but also encouraging, particularly when he felt inferior to the others because of his exclusions or physical limitations (compared to the others). It didn't matter what he did – bump into a large dolphin, get out of synch with the others as they surfaced to breathe, fail to corral fish during feeding – he could always count on a big, forgiving smile, even if he was snouted as a result. In many ways, those smiles reminded him of his Grandpa's crooked, shaky smile, and the way that he could love and forgive endlessly.

"I love you, sport," he could remember his Grandpa saying to him, after which the old man would pat him on the head with a touch that was soft and shaky.

"I love you, too, Grandpa, more than anything in the world."

XIII

The months and years passed. He swam the world's great oceans with the others, and he continued to grow and mature until by his own estimation he was able to keep up with most of the dolphins, no matter where they were or how abruptly they turned. He still couldn't comprehend the reasons for their movements, but at least he was now capable of catching up with them when need be and he didn't worry when they got a little way in front of him. Over time, he had also gained a nickname. The name, which was impossible to pronounce, consisted of six long clicks, followed by seventy-five short clicks enunciated in three short bursts of twenty-five clicks each. Everyone else had a name, which he was generally able to pronounce with varying degrees of success, although for some reason he often confused the names of one large female and one even larger male (he could tell by they way they turned when he called to them). No one was particularly bothered by these and other slips – not even the dolphins whose identities he had confused – which was demonstrated by their longsuffering attitudes and benevolent smiles.

Over time, he had also gained a modicum of wisdom, which had come from living a fair amount of time and making an even fairer amount of mistakes and, of course, learning from his mistakes. He still wasn't perfect, but in his wisdom he recognized – and accepted – his lack of perfection and, equally important, he continued to do his very best to rise above and conquer anything that made him less than the dolphin he was meant to be. One very important aspect of this wisdom was understanding the importance of being "one" with the group – being, when necessary, a mirror image of everyone else as they sailed through the waters from place to place or, especially, over the dark, seemingly uninhabited open seas. Breathing in unison with the others (still the only movement that he could accurately predict) was a critical aspect of this oneness, but so were feeding, hunting, traveling, and swarming. Swarming, so crucial for defense, was the process of moving tightly together so that those strange animals from the black depths beyond the reef couldn't identify a point of weakness to attack any single dolphin. (Swarming also confused certain feeble-minded predators, who appeared convinced that the dolphin swarm was an animal too large to attack.) But swarming wasn't the only action critical to the dolphins' preservation – the dolphins also needed to be able to act in concert to warn others of possible dangers or, if the dangers were apparent, undertake a variety of evasive maneuvers, only some of which included swarming. Surprisingly, there were far more threats to dolphins than he had imagined when he first slipped under the water's surface, and even with his increasing wisdom, he was constantly learning of new dangers that could bring his life to an abrupt end.

One day, when the water was warm and the golden light above began to retreat toward the horizon, the dolphins were close to a beach on the other side of the world, or at least it seemed like it because it resembled no beach that he had ever seen. It was little more than a narrow strip of brown sand that was blocked off from the rest of the land by sharp, rugged cliffs that were home to thousands of screeching gulls and little else. The dolphins had apparently come to the area because of warm waters and the plentiful supply of food (one didn't have to work to find something edible). Since the land was deserted and there were few predators trolling the waters, the group stayed in the area for several days, eating and jumping, diving, racing, and playing a myriad of games whose rules and goals he couldn't begin to understand. Ultimately, it proved to be one of the most enjoyable periods of his life, particularly because one of the largest dolphins – an animal nearly a foot longer than most of the others – decided to play a series of games with him.

Most of the games were challenges of one sort or another, pitting the larger dolphin's mental acuity against his younger, seemingly more agile physical abilities. One challenge was to find out who was quickest from the ocean floor (the water at that point was only about thirty feet deep) to the surface, while another was to see who could reach the surface and return with the smallest splash. He performed respectably, but he realized too late that the other dolphin had tricked him by touching bottom at a shallower point, which enabled it to reach the surface first and, because only its dorsal fin touched the air, it hardly disturbed a single drop of water. He, too, smiled when the dolphin nudged him in the side or stomach with its hard snout every time he came up short in their contests. They continued to play this particular game – and each time he came up short for one reason or another – until the sun began to touch the horizon, sending shimmering golden rays across the surface of the water. He had expected to continue the games for some time after this (or until he had taken at least one conquest) when the dolphin suddenly broke away and began swimming out across the deep waters, the depths of which were now completely black.

He didn't know what had happened. The dolphin's behavior was peculiar – it almost seemed like the animal was deliberately putting itself at risk – and he couldn't help wondering if he had done something wrong, broken some unwritten rule, that offended the animal and caused it to swim away. He glanced around hoping to find the answer, and when he couldn't see anything that might suggest a cause for the animal's behavior, he decided to follow it, hoping that its actions signaled a new game or some other kind of activity.

He followed the animal for some time. He stayed close enough to keep it in sight, but not so close that it would notice his presence or suspect that it was being followed. While he continued to worry that his relations with the dolphin may have been damaged, he was nevertheless pleased that he could easily keep pace with the much larger animal, not only demonstrating his physical prowess but also highlighting the fact that he had become strong enough to keep up with one of the strongest and cleverest swimmers in the group. Indeed, the longer he followed the dolphin without getting tired or physically stressed, the more he began to feel that he was truly one of them and possessed the same strengths, agility, and cunning. In a sense, he felt that he had come of age in this beautiful undersea world, even though at the moment he was traveling over dark, open waters. But just as all these things were going through his head, the dolphin suddenly picked up speed and, pushing his tail furiously up and down against the currents, started to pull away from him, increasing the distance between the two every second. In response, he doubled his speed as well, and for a minute or so he thought that he might actually catch up or at least keep pace with the animal, but his hope quickly faded when, despite his best efforts, the dolphin again increased both his speed and the distance between the two. He tried moving his own tail and body in unison with the dolphin, hoping that this would at least keep him close enough so that he wouldn't lose sight of the dolphin, but even this didn't work and he continued to fall behind, especially when he was forced to break the surface for air. Each time he returned from the surface, the dolphin seemed to be even farther ahead (inexplicably, the animal never seemed to need air, or else it surfaced when he wasn't looking). He didn't give up, however, and continued to push himself until his sides were sore and his lungs nearly bursting – he didn't want to end up alone over the dark waters below.

The dolphin was hardly more than a dim spec in the fading light, when he felt a nudge against his sides and saw that all the others were swimming with him, all apparently following the same dolphin. For a moment, he was relieved because it no longer mattered if he lost sight of the dolphin (and, by this point, he had); equally important, he was glad to have some company, especially as the night crept around him and the dark waters moved closer and closer to where he was swimming. Unfortunately, his relief was short lived, because as he looked back and forth at his companions, he noticed that they, too, were swimming with an unusual determination and, although they continued smiling, they were doing nothing to ensure that he kept up with them and was not lost. In fact, they ignored him, and as they moved forward with a speed that he couldn't match (no doubt because he had overextended himself following the other dolphin), he began to fall behind and in no time they were disappearing into the same encroaching darkness that had swallowed the other dolphin. He still didn't give up, as he might have done in a similar situation on land (as he had done many times when outmatched in physical contests), and continued on in their wake, using every ounce of energy he had left to ensure that he didn't lose them.

He was on the verge of collapse when they unexpectedly slowed and quickly came back into sight. Only a few yards in front of him they had slowed down in front of a strange, pulsating black ball. At first, there was no way of telling how big it was (the dark ball initially seemed small, like a volley ball or a basketball), but the closer he got to it the more it increased in size until it was larger than just about anything he had ever seen before. He had seen balls of fish before – balls so big that they were many dolphins high and equally many wide – but none of them matched the size of this ball and none were as jam-packed with millions of small, glowing fish as this one. Balls of fish were always fun, because it was easy to swim through them and eat mouthfuls of fish with little or no effort. As soon as he caught up with the others, he noticed that they all seemed to be hesitating, as if they were waiting for a signal from the large dolphin before launching themselves into the ball.

He, too, waited, perhaps thirty feet from the ball, for the large dolphin to make his move. Eying the others for signs that they were ready to move, he cause sight of the large dolphin, which suddenly charged toward the ball, veering upward and around it just before reaching it. The dolphin flew out of the water and seconds later appeared in the ball with the other fish. Feeding greedily on the fish, the animal jerked this way and then that, filling his belly and sating his animal energies until something peculiar happened. As he and the others watched, the large dolphin began shivering and shaking its entire body in a way which suggested that it had either become violently ill or stark, raving mad. Within seconds, the dolphin's movements had become so wild and violent that he involuntarily moved backward a few feet, refusing to go anywhere near the ball, even when four of the others flew out of the water and dove into the ball. Seconds after this, they, too, began to show symptoms of the strange affliction that had come over the large dolphin.

He didn't know what to do, nor, for that matter, did the other dolphins, which hovered around the ball, watching their disturbing antics but not daring to move any closer, much less enter the ball with the others. Unconsciously, he had begun to inch closer to some of the others outside of the ball for security (and possibly for some clue as to what was happening) when something strange and unexpected began to happen to the ball – it started to rise, moving slowly toward the surface in short, abrupt jerks that elongated its circular shape, until the top finally reached the surface and then, in a single violent, upward leap, the ball disappeared, along with the dolphins eating it. It didn't take long for everyone to understand the neither the ball nor the dolphins trapped inside it would ever return. With no other reason to stay, and every reason to hasten away, they turned and headed back to the reef and safe waters. This time he had no trouble keeping up with them.

The following day was bright and sunny, and the intense light of the sun filtered down through the water in softly drifting flakes of gold. It was also one of the most troubling days he had ever experienced. While everyone smiled and acted as if yesterday had never happened, there was no playing or hunting throughout the entire day; the group stayed close together and moved swiftly through the water, never resting and never allowing any one to move more than a few inches from the others. The one time that he tried to get out of synch and catch a breath of air, he was forced back into the group by dozens of hard, bony snouts, and nearly passed out from the lack of air until the group moved as one to the surface, breathed in unison, and then returned to the depths and continued their procession to safety, which arrived as the dawn arrived and the terrors of the night dissipated into the dark recesses of the group's memory. He was sore for days afterwards, although he was comforted by the fact that never once during this entire incident did anyone cease smiling.

XIV

He hoped that in time he would make fewer mistakes. Even if he was never able to anticipate their actions, he thought that he could at least learn enough to prevent some of his most egregious errors and, over time, become a highly functional, dependable member of the group. Human beings have a similar problem – it takes time for a young adult to overcome ignorance and immaturity – and yet no matter how long he lived among the others, no matter how many times he engaged in this or that activity with them, there was always something that he didn't know, something that unfortunately he would have to learn the hard way. It was embarrassing that after living with them and learning so many things, he continued to make mistake after mistake, after mistake. None of the others seemed to make so many mistakes, even the young ones who were less than half his size, and it continued on and on, month after month, year after year without let up. At times, his head ached after doing something singularly stupid, and then he would have to muster every ounce of his strength just to continue on and not give up, like he might have done in a previous life. Take fishing, for instance. He hunted fish with them every day and even though his skills and expertise seemed to improve every day, he invariably made a large, costly error, such as positioning himself in the wrong direction to corral small fish, thus enabling them to escape around him, often right in front of his nose. To make matters worse, when his hunger was particularly intense, he would sometimes forget his obligations to the others and eat some of the fish that he did corner instead of leaving them to dolphins too old or young to catch fish on their own. Naturally, his actions would not go unnoticed, and he would end up with several sharp, unexpected pokes to the belly until he disgorged the fish and allowed their rightful owners to take possession.

Early on, playtime offered a respite from his troubles, but after a while even this failed to provide him the joy he expected from dolphin life. When he was younger, he treasured play time, because it consisted of many of the same kinds of games he played when he was on land, albeit with modifications to suit the underwater environment. But as he got older, he lost his interest in many of these activities, since there was little variety in dolphin games, and everyone no matter how big or small seemed inordinately fond of repeating the same game over and over, often forgoing food and other, more important activities in order to repeat the same movements, the same activities until…well, sometimes there never seemed to be an end to them unless some event or threat intervened. One of the best games was a swimming challenge. Instead of diving down and touching the ocean floor and then breaching the surface, one swam from point A (perhaps a lump of coral) to point B (perhaps another lump of coral) as fast as one could and back again. It was fun because it challenged the muscles and helped him understand his strengths and cunning compared to everyone else; but the game soon lost most of its allure when he realized that its true and only purpose was to swim from one point to another, and back again. There were no winners, because it was never clear when the game started and when it ended. Then there was leaping, which was little more than leaping into the air and diving, nose first, back into the water. This, too, was initially fun, but repeating the same movements over and over quickly became monotonous, and when he played he couldn't help wishing that something would happen to vary the game and break the monotony. The appearance of a boat sometimes helped, but after a while even this became boring because the only thing anyone wanted to do was to keep abreast of the boat for an unspecified period of time. There were other games, but he avoided most of these because the participants, mainly the larger males, would poke and bite each other while the females would slowly circle and observe the action. Later on, the games did little to distract him from his problems (such as doing something stupid), which would be waiting for him when the games were thankfully and mercifully over.

Maybe it would have been better – maybe he could have soothed his fears and anxieties – by talking about these things with one of the older dolphins. They all loved talking -- clicking, whistling, shrieking, going on nonstop from dawn to dusk and ceasing only in times of danger or when swimming in the deep, open water at night – but they didn't talk to him. Well, they did talk, but unfortunately he couldn't understand everything that they were telling him, and his ability to respond was limited, too. He could click and squeak like the best of them, but for some reason what he wanted to communicate in clicks and shrieks must have seemed like gibberish, judging by the way they sometimes paused, shook their heads, and then turned away. There were times, certainly, that they could all communicate fairly effectively – especially when there was danger or when someone spotted food – but normal, casual conversation was practically impossible, even when he really needed someone to talk to. Maybe conversation of this sort was best done by humans, or maybe by the time one truly became integrated into dolphin society one didn't need such conversations.

Sometimes, when he felt especially sad or troubled, images from his past would involuntarily creep up into his mind. He often recalled conversations with his Grandpa, but he also recalled important conversations with his friends and school mates. Larry, the boy who lived across the street, was a great sounding board for his problems, and the two of them together could easily solve the most intractable problems.

"I don't want to go home," he once said to Larry, while the two of them were playing in a shallow cave in an abandoned field about a mile from where they both lived.

"Neither do I," Larry responded.

"Let's stay here."

"Okay."

"Forever."

"Okay, but I have to be back home before dinner."

"Me, too."

"So what else do you want to do?"

"I don't know."

"Me, either."

Still, he wouldn't have changed this life for his life back on land. Even during the worst times here, there was always joy, love, and camaraderie. There was also freedom, the ability to explore and leave the things that one didn't like or were hurtful. Of course, there were important boundaries that should never be crossed (such as straying from the group), but these were minor inconveniences compared to the problems inherent in land life, which was little more than limits, prohibitions, and warnings. And punishments. He was always being punished for something, or else he was forbidden to do something, even if that something was enjoyable and completely harmless. Even then, he could have tolerated all of it if he could have seen his Grandpa more often. Grandpa was the only one who completely understood how life worked, the only one who knew how to avoid many of the strictures that could make living uncomfortable; plus, he was the only one who loved him unconditionally, even after one or more of his many failures – not even the love from the others was as great as his Grandpa's love. Truly, apart from Grandpa, the only individuals who offered a respite from typical human interactions were Larry and a few other friends. When he was with Larry, he could make noise, get dirty, and connect with the earth in ways that were forbidden elsewhere, especially at home. He especially remembered those times when he and Larry would sneak out to the cave where, away from the harsh glare of adults' eyes, they would all dig into the moist, red earth inside the cave with their bare hands. Few things in this world were as pleasurable as holding the soil in your hands, feeling your fingers tickle as it sifted back toward the earth, and absorbing its cool, musty smell every time it was disturbed.

"What are you doing, Larry?" he asked, as Larry inevitably crushed the soil in his hands and then rubbed it into the tops of his pants.

"Nothing," Larry would just as invariably reply, "just getting dirty. What are you doing?"

"Just getting dirty," he would say with a smile as large as any dolphin's and then smear the dirt and clay on his pants, too.

By the time he got home, he was pretty dirty, which would occasion warnings and complaints from his mother about his clothes, the house, the carpets, and everything else. Cold weather put a damper on the cave, but he and Larry could always find other things to do, and there were even times when he didn't mind being alone. He did miss the cave and Larry and, sometimes, even his own room, but he still wouldn't have exchanged it for life in the sea and with the dolphins. Never, even if he sometimes wondered what it would be like to visit Larry and the rest of his past life from time to time.

XV

These were good years, and life under water was more pleasant than anything he had experienced on land. Sure, he missed Grandpa, Larry, and others, as well as the cave, his room, his toys, his school, and a few other things, but in their place he had new friends (more or less), dolphins who loved him, and he possessed the ability to explore the most extraordinary world imaginable. Despite his years under the water, he was still amazed by everything around him – the brilliant colors, the strange fish, and his sleek companions, who never failed to display their affection for him through warm, approving smiles – and he almost never regretted having left dry land; and he was also certain that if he ever had a chance to return to the world he had once inhabited, he would have rejected it and would have swum as far away from land as he could go, even if it meant swimming across the deep waters at night. Naturally, this didn't mean that he was willing to discard the memories that floated around in his head. On the contrary, he wanted to keep most of those forever, because if nothing else they reminded him of his great luck in finding this new world, which he had no intention of abandoning. Still, he would have given almost anything to go back for a few days to walk where his Grandpa had walked, to touch the things that he had touched, and to breathe the same air that he had breathed; even if none of this could bring the old man back to life, it would have been enough to evoke his presence just long enough so that it would never be lost no matter how long he lived or how far away from his Grandpa's world that he traveled.

Not long after this, he began to experience an odd, unsettling sensation. The group had been feeding off a shallow reef that ended near a long, narrow beach. The beach was delineated by high sands dunes and, nestled in between them, dozens of old Victorian houses. Neither the beach nor the dunes seemed particularly special, but every time that he surfaced for air and caught sight of the area, something inside him stirred and he would begin to wonder who the people on the beach were and what they were doing as they crowded around one small section at the edge of the water. It was impossible to get close enough, and so he did what he could to follow their movements (still staying with the group) until it was time to move farther down the reef. The following day, they had come back to the same area, and the same scene again presented itself, people crowding around a small spot just off the water and...well, he still couldn't tell what they were doing. Shortly after this, the group again moved on, only to come back the next day and, surprisingly, the same thing was happening on the beach, with what appeared to be the same small group of people bouncing up and down, hollering, and who knows what else. The group stayed off shore for most of the day before heading down the coast for warmer waters, which they planned to inhabit for the rest of the season. Throughout the entire day, the people clustering around the small area hardly ever moved. Sure, some people ran from one or two of the houses to join them, and occasionally someone ran off toward one of the other houses, but by and large the people stayed there, bent over something on the sand or in the shallowest part of the water. His interested wasn't piqued by the peculiarity of this behavior but by the fact that every time he noticed this scene, he was filled with an inexplicable foreboding, as if something unfortunate was happening to those people and he was powerless to stop it. It didn't make sense, and so he was glad that the others eventually moved past the area.

The following day, the group rested at another section of the coast, perhaps a hundred miles farther south. This section of the beach looked similar to the other section, except that there were no houses in sight and the humans were scattered across the beach, not clumped in one small section. The humans here, unlike the humans on the other beach, were all engaged in some kind of activity, either by themselves or in small groups -- some were lying on the sand, some were walking along the edge of the water, some were digging holes and building sand castles, some were throwing balls and other objects, and many of them were in the water either splashing at the edge where the water washed ashore or swimming farther out, sometimes with rubber tubes or fiberglass boards – and he was surprised by the differences between the humans on the two beaches. In his mind, there was no logical reason why the people should behave so differently on what was essentially the same stretch of sand, since humans were humans no matter where they were. For days after that, long after they had departed from this section of the coast, he continued to think about the behavior of the humans, wondering why their behavior should be so different on what was essentially the same stretch of sand. Moreover, every time he considered the humans on the beach with the Victorian houses, he couldn't help feeling that something must be wrong and that whatever it was, it could have disastrous implications for the dolphins.

It was deeply troubling to have this kind of knowledge and not be able to tell anyone. He tried to say something to the older dolphins – several times – and yet every time he approached them, he was unable to deliver his message. The problem was that he had no definitive information, and so he feared that if he articulated these vague forebodings, they would smile at him and either ignore him or marvel at his ability to create fantasies out of thin air. Then again, because he had had so much trouble with the language, there was a good chance that he would mangle the language so much that they wouldn't understand anything he said. Fortunately, his anxiety over both the situation on the beach and his inability to articulate the problem faded over time due to the flurry of activities (and games) that began to occupy his body and his mind -- fish were suddenly abundant, and the group needed to fill their stomachs before crossing the waters to another continent, and they also needed to be on the lookout for predators, which often patrolled such waters because they knew the dolphins would be feeding at such places. However, once they were finally traveling and no longer concerned with all the preparations for the trip, he had settled into a routine of swimming and breathing that not only relaxed his mind but also allowed the strange thoughts to creep back into his mind. This time, though, his anxieties over the humans on the beach had faded, although he couldn't help thinking about human life, particularly his own life so many years ago.

These weren't grand thoughts about living and dying, just memories of what it was like to be human and what it was like to be a little boy, surrounded by his toys, his friends, and even his mom and Bob. He wondered, for example, what it would be like to have his toys again – things that belonged to him alone, things that he didn't have to share with anyone else – and to sleep in a large bed again, surrounded by his stuffed animals and near a tall bookcase that contained most of his books (the large dolphin book would still be under his bed for safe keeping). Sleeping in the water was a wonderful sensation, since you are always comfortable and never have to toss and turn to settle in just right; but there was also something indescribably pleasant about sleeping in one's own bed, which was not only warm and comfortable but also secure, a place in which he could withdraw into a world of his own making that stood apart from all the other worlds created and controlled by adults. He missed this aspect of human life, and as far as he knew there was no way to recreate these sensations under the water's surface. But he also missed lying in bed in the morning while he waited for the alarm to sound, the taste of his mother's breakfasts and her admonitions to eat more so that he wouldn't be hungry during the day, and the school bus that would take him and the other children to school, where they would spend the day reading and calculating, and all the stuff that he had once taken for granted. And he missed going home at night and seeing all the familiar things that were once part of his life, and everything else in its proper place, unless of course his mother was cleaning that day. He missed his mom, even when she was frustrated with him, and he missed Bob a little, too. He might have missed his Dad more, if only he could have remembered what he looked like. More than anything else, though, he missed his Grandpa, especially during those times when he would sneak a cookie into his room late at night after his mother or Bob denied him that very same cookie, or when the old man would whisper to him that his mother was wrong for having scolded him for something or deprived him of his cookie.

He wanted to explain these feelings to some of the others, because he knew that talking about them sometimes made him feel better, and he also knew that one or two of the older ones would know the right things to say in response, just like his mom sometimes knew the right things to say or his Grandpa, who always knew what he was thinking and always had the very words he needed to feel better or good about himself. But even if the dolphins could say the right things, it was doubtful that he could make himself understood well enough to elicit their responses, and it was equally doubtful that if they did understand him he could understand them.

64

Besides, how could he describe the sensation of a bed or toys when they had never seen much less experienced a bed or his ranger toys; and how could they be expected to make sense of the concept of friends when they didn't have friends like those he left behind in the human world? How could he make them understand how special Larry was or Johnny Wilson? Johnny Wilson was a boy his age who lived in the neighborhood and whose house was the locus of so many wonderful toys and pastimes (his father was a science teacher, and so the Wilson house was filled with all kinds of amazing tools and gadgets, including a telescope that rose higher than any adult in the neighborhood, a magnifying glass that was as big around as a dinner plate, and sunglasses that enabled one to look directly at the sun without being blinded, and so many other things that were useless under water), and he spent many hours there playing with Johnny and these things, which were unknown and unintelligible even to the most knowledgeable of dolphins. Or dirt and mud? What was mud and dirt to a dolphin? How could he explain birthdays, holidays, or Christmas, the one time during the year when his mother and Bob seemed genuinely fond of Grandpa, who would either call or visit and who could be counted on to provide lots of presents and edible treats such as cookies and cakes. And then there was the yard behind his house with his swing set and wooden playhouse; the closely-cut lawn that covered most of the ground in the yard and that smelled wonderful whenever it was cut during the summer; the giant trees that filled the park and the leaves blanketed the park and even his back yard in autumn; and his school with its long blacktop, grass-covered playground, and monkey bars and slides, which couldn't be used during summer because they heated up like frying pans and burnt everything that touched them. Even if he had words or clicks that would have enabled him to describe and explain these things, there was no way that he could describe or explain his feelings, and so there was no way that they could find the right words that would ease the discomfort in his stomach or stop his increasing longing to go home to his mom and Bob and the memory of his Grandpa.

He was often able to set aside these thoughts when necessities demanded, but he was never able to discard completely the soft, gnawing feeling in his stomach that sometimes made him wonder if he was sick. But he was sick, sick from the desire to go back home, to go back to the place where everything was familiar and comfortable, where he could feel the same sensations as all the other children in his neighborhood and in his class at school, to be at school, where he could think about his home and long to be either at recess or on his way home, even if he had homework due the next day. Yes, the more he thought about it, the more he missed his mother and Bob, for if nothing else they represented home, even if the home they represented was not the one he would have created had he the ability to do so. He was certain that they liked him and that all the rules and regulations, all the prohibitions, all the demands to do this and that before Bob came home or so his mother wouldn't be disappointed, were for his own good, so that he wouldn't become worthless when he grew up. Perhaps he was worthless, because he had gone to the beach after he had been forbidden to do so and had doubtless forced his mother and Bob to come looking for him, only to leave the beach shore empty handed. He sometimes wondered how they had handled his absence and whether his mother had cried when she learned that she would be returning home without him. His mother cried very easily. Once she even cried after he had soiled his pants. On certain days, when the necessities of food and security seemed remote, he sometimes wished to be punished for his transgression of leaving home, if only…if only he could take his punishment at home.

Going home was impossible. Even if he were to swim back to the beach (if, indeed, he could find it – having seen so many beaches since that time, he wasn't sure that he could distinguish one from another), he was certain that his mom and Bob were long gone. Even if by some strange coincidence they were still there, perhaps living in the same beach house and, from time to time, visiting the very spot where he disappeared – even if by some even stranger coincidence they were to catch sight of him offshore, spotting him watching them, would they recognize him? He had changed so much over the years, enough to become unrecognizable to everyone he once knew, although he couldn't quite tell how much because he lacked a mirror to examine himself. And if they did, would they be willing to let him back in, someone who was now a complete stranger? Perhaps they had consoled themselves over his loss by having another child, one who was more obedient and who didn't cause them so much trouble and pain.

It was this, the realization that he could never return home, that troubled him month after month, year after year, so that he gradually lost the energy and the will to play with the others, despite the fact that they never lost the desire to be friendly with him. One time he was so despondent that he could barely rouse himself to go to the surface to take a necessary breath of air. Had it not been for the rest of the group, and their bony-nosed insistence that he return to the surface with the rest of them, he might have drowned.

XVI

Not long after this, they came to a different reef and proceeded to do all the things that they normally did at every other reef. Naturally, he had come with the group, but for some time his enthusiasm for dolphin activities had flagged somewhat, and instead of jumping in and participating wholeheartedly with the others in whatever they were doing, he held back and swam around the reef listlessly, wondering what it would be like to be home after so much time away. While he was imagining what home was like and if anything had changed, he suddenly felt uneasy, as if there was danger nearby. He didn't immediately see the source of danger as he looked around, but after a few moments he noticed that no one was in sight – there wasn't a single dolphin anywhere and, what's more, he couldn't detect a single trace of them, not a sound, smell, or remnant from feeding. In many ways, it was a shocking realization, because he had never been anywhere in the water without at least one dolphin nearby.

He didn't panic. He carefully scanned the waters in every direction and, failing to find them, began darting back and forth across the reef, hoping to catch sight of one or more of them or, if nothing else, to pick up a trace of something that might indicate where they were traveling. But there was nothing, not a single thing to suggest that they had ever been to this reef. It didn't make sense. They must have begun moving somewhere (how else could their absence be explained?), but since he didn't know which direction they may have taken, he decided to stay put for the time being and wait for them to come back for him. They wouldn't forget him, and if he moved in the wrong direction, they might have trouble finding him. While he waited, he promised himself that he would never again lose sight of the others, even if he had to keep his eyes on them at all times.

But one minute passed and then another, and he began to fear that they might not know where to look for him or, what was worse, that they might not yet know that he was missing, which would increase the distance between them before they turned to find him – and at some point that distance could be so great that they might never find him. Compounding the problem was the fact that the water all around him had become eerily silent; nothing, not even the soft, muffled hush of an underwater wave could be heard. He had never experienced anything so quiet in his life, which not only made him more uneasy but also made him feel completely alone, because he knew that under normal circumstances, with the sounds of waves crashing overhead and the chatter of all the other animals in the deep, he still could have communicated with his companions from a distance of at least ten miles away. In water as quiet as it was now, he could have heard them half an ocean away, which could mean that they were now so far away that he would never be found.

He didn't know what to do. He hadn't been taught what to do in a situation like this. Sure, dolphins disappeared from time to time, but that was generally due to poor health or death, which was usually the same thing, but no one in good health ever got lost. Not until now, at least. This, too, weighed on his nerves until he decided that the best thing he could do under the circumstances was to look for the others and not wait for them to find him. It was a bold decision, but what else could he do?

He immediately breached the surface and inhaled huge gasps of air that filled and refreshed him like a good meal. Without the others to goad him, he had nearly forgotten to take in some air, and as a result his lungs ached. At least the water was smooth, and so he was in a good position to scan its surface for any telltale signs of the group. But the surface yielded no clues as to the others' whereabouts. Undeterred, he decided to swim in a direction that they might be traveling and catch up with them. As he slipped back beneath the surface, he noticed that the water was becoming increasingly murky.

Not knowing where they had been heading (and he regretted having paid insufficient attention to them when they began to signal their intentions, assuming that he could have understood what they were), he took off in a direction that seemed reasonable. Breaching the surface and greedily inhaling one more time, he dove back under the surface and began swimming furiously. He pushed his body through the cool waters with all his might, breaching the surface from time to time not only to inhale the precious air, but also to look for anything familiar on the horizon. He also breached frequently because it allowed him to move faster, the air lacking the resistance inherent in the water. Occasionally, he would pause, poke his head out of the water to look for signs of the others, click several times to make sure that they could hear him even if they couldn't see him, and then, when it was clear that he was still alone in an endless sea of nothing, move onward, pushing himself relentlessly to locate the others.

One time when he breached the surface, he thought he saw a small fin protruding out of the water, and so he headed into the direction, hoping that at last he had found all the others. However, when he reached the spot where the fin might have been, he was disappointed to see nothing there, not even the faintest trace of something that could have indicated the presence of dolphins. This made him think that it might have been a distant sail, and so he continued swimming in the same direction, knowing that it was easy to locate a slow-moving sailboat. If it was a sailboat, then at least he knew that he wasn't alone, and it might even attract the attention of the others, if they were nearby, who would be certain to swim toward the boat to play with it.

He turned and began swimming in the direction of the sailboat. He didn't know how long he had been swimming – it seemed like days, even weeks, although it was perhaps only a few hours – with nothing more than a vague shape in his mind's eye, when he finally slowed and hesitated. This time, as he had done several times along the way, he looked around for signs of the sail, but there was nothing except an endless stretch of smooth, motionless water, and of course the silence.

The failure to find the boat, the useless waste of time chasing after what was probably a mirage, filled him with an anger at himself that had he been on land, he would have pulled at his hair and ripped his shirt off. Instead, he floated on the surface and thrashed his head back and forth, remonstrating with himself but oddly thankful that at least his exertions made a sound in this strangely silent world. Perhaps the worst of it was not the loss of time or the folly of having chased a mirage, but the fact that he could no longer remember where he had been when he first noticed his isolation. Breaching the surface and peering into the dead space that surrounded him, he struggled to understand what was best to do under the circumstances. He also wondered where his next meal would be found. All the effort of looking for the others and the phantom boat made his stomach raw with hunger, and unfortunately there was still nothing at all in sight that could be eaten.

With a heavy heart and an empty stomach, and filled with a fear of all the possible dangers that awaited him while he was separated from the others, he decided to continue on in the same direction that he had been swimming.

XVII

The sun was beginning to set, and just as its bottom edge touched the horizon, it appeared to explode and filled the sky with a dazzling array of golds, yellows, reds, and oranges. These same electric colors also covered the surface of the water, dissolving the horizon and making the water seem like a fiery extension of the sky. Ordinarily, the sight of such an extraordinary sunset would have imbued him with joy and hopefulness, but on this occasion it only elicited dread, because he knew it would be dark soon and this would compound the difficulty of finding the others and returning to safer waters. Fearing the prospect that awaited him, he started to arch his back and dip his nose toward the water when he suddenly caught sight of something out the corner of his eyes.

It couldn't have been more than a few yards to his right. It was long and sleek, and, as it slipped behind him and out of sight, the sun's dying light glimmered off its surface the same way that it would have glimmered off the back of a dolphin. The possibility that he had indeed seen another dolphin – maybe even the others – made his heart leap and arrested his movement, but no sooner had he turned to his right than it was gone and in its place was nothing but water, now growing darker and duller by the second as the sun started to sink behind the horizon.

He couldn't believe it. He was positive that he had seen something (and it was quite reasonable, he assured himself, that he had caught a glimpse of a dolphin, for what other animal would have breached the surface like that and at this very moment?), and yet as he stared in the direction of where the shape should have been, there wasn't even the slightest ripple to suggest that anything had actually touched the water. It didn't make sense and, suddenly concerned that he may have been deceived a second time, he carefully scanned the surface of the water in all directions, looking for signs of either the shape or the others. Seconds passed and then minutes, but there was nothing to quell his fears that he had made another mistake, and so he dropped beneath the surface and began darting back and forth in the dark water, searching for something, anything, that might have been the shape he had seen. But, again, there was nothing – nothing either as big as a dolphin or as small as a shrimp within a few hundred yards in any direction – and so he stopped and, moving his tail back and forth, turned around and around trying to locate something and wondering, at the same time, if he had seen anything at all or if all these shapes and sailboats were nothing more than delusions created by a brain feverish with fear and loneliness.

Sick from turning around and quickly running out of air, he stopped moving and, setting the issue of his mental health aside, he began listlessly paddling upward, back to the surface.

He still remembered the summer before his Grandpa passed away. Grandpa had arrived in a blaze of glory like the setting sun, and, after securing his mother's reluctant agreement, he and the old gentleman went camping in the back yard. It was a great adventure, especially because he had never been camping before and because his Grandpa had dedicated the entire evening to him. As they huddled together in beach chairs watching shadowy creatures dance across the red and orange embers dying in a small BBQ, his Grandpa told him about the facts of life in the sea after sunset. "Listen, my boy, it's a deadly world outside once the sun goes down," he began with embers reflecting off his craggy old face, making it look more like a burning ember than his loving Grandpa's face. "When that happens, most sea creatures do their best to hide until first light. I remember once sitting on the beach at night, just like you and I are sitting here, and hearing the moans of suffering creatures big and small floating across the water." He starred at him intently to make his point. "The moans were moans of destitution, because no one was coming to their aid. At the same time, I could see the phosphorescence traces of predators flashing on the waves as these fish chased their prey to their deaths or insanity." His old arms sliced through the air to mimic the movements of the predatory fish. He smiled after this and a few moments after this, laughed with his typical deep, shaking bark, at the same time giving him a big bear hug which practically smothered him but which thrilled him to the core.

"I'm only telling you a story," he said. "You're supposed to tell scary stories over a campfire, or didn't anyone ever do that? I suppose you've never been camping."

"This is the first time, remember?" It didn't matter whether his Grandpa remembered or not, because he couldn't imagine a better campfire, even with the occasional tepid spark floating up and disappearing into the dark night.

"But let me tell you something else," Grandpa continued, this time holding him at arm's length. "It can be a dangerous world both in nature and in our human world. But you and I have each other, and so there's nothing anywhere that will ever harm you – and if it does, you tell me immediately." He smiled again, gave him another bear hug, and then sat back while they enjoyed the darkness and the glow of the BBQ. Later on, the old man was crestfallen that he had forgotten to bring skewers for roasting marshmallows. He had also forgotten to bring marshmallows, but that didn't seem to trouble him as much.

His reverie ended when he thought he saw the same, sleek shape that he had seen earlier. Once again, it crossed the periphery of his vision on his right side and then disappeared, this time like the last leaving no telltale trace of its murky existence in the dark waters. His past experience, as well as the brevity of the shape's sighting, didn't infuse him with confidence that he had actually seen anything other than perhaps another wave or apparition in his mind, and yet he couldn't completely discard the image, especially if there was the slightest chance that it was another dolphin. He had to check it out. Besides, what else was there to do? He could stay where he was and hope that someone (or something) would find him, but it seemed unlikely now that the sun had disappeared and the others would probably be reluctant to fan out (especially over deep waters) in search of someone who got lost because he hadn't been paying attention to the group like everyone else. No, at this moment, locating the others was entirely up to him, and while it would have been better to have searched during the day, he no longer had the luxury – alone at night and over deep waters was the last place that any dolphin wanted to be.

Shaking his head to clear his thoughts, he raced to the surface one more time to fill his lungs with air and, after slipping back beneath the surface, he looked around carefully to see if another dolphin was in sight. Not surprisingly, he didn't see anything (it was so dark that he couldn't see more than a few feet in any direction). He also tried clicking and squeaking, but these didn't return a response except for some muffled, unrecognizable sounds from somewhere in the depths below. With nothing left to try or do, he turned toward the direction he thought the shape had been moving and began swimming. He was a little hesitant at first, but he quickly picked up speed and was soon moving as swiftly as he had during the day.

He swam with his usual confidence, despite the fact that he wasn't entirely certain that he was going in the right direction or what he would do when he didn't find the shape or became exhausted (normally, he could swim steadily for hours on end, but he was moving a little faster than normal and so there was a real chance that he would tire and be forced to stop). But after a while, his confidence began to flag because he was traveling over deep waters and the moon still had not risen. The moon was truly the only thing that could protect him on a night like this, because it could illuminate the water near the surface enough to keep most of the denizens from venturing up to where he was swimming. A couple of times he breached the surface for air and to see if the moon was hiding behind clouds and hence would soon light up the waters, and each time he was disappointed, for it was nowhere to be seen, and dark clouds filled the sky so that even if the moon were in the sky, it was doubtful that its light would penetrate the clouds. His disappointment in not finding the moon, and his fear that he was only chasing a figment of his imagination, soon intensified and he became concerned that he was traveling in the wrong direction. He couldn't have explained it even to himself, but he suddenly realized that everything he was doing was contrary to what he should be doing and that, as a result, he needed to turn around immediately and head for shallow waters. Because night sometimes makes the most complex options simple, he decided that he would go to some place safe to wait out the night; at dawn, he promised himself, he would continue the search.

Stopping and turning around, he headed back toward the direction he thought he would find shallow water.

XVIII

He swam for what seemed like hours without coming any closer to shallower water than he had been in when he decided to turn away from the shape. He didn't really know how long he had been swimming (he had long ago lost a human's sense of time), but it seemed like hours, maybe even more. He hoped that it wasn't longer, because that might suggest that the moonless darkness was an unnatural state that might never end. But at least he kept close to the surface during this time. The surface was the safest place to be, and it had the advantage of letting him know up from down, especially as the water broke over his back.

There were, however, a couple of other times when he was almost certain that he had seen the shape again, but like every other time when he turned to look, it was gone and he was left wondering if he had imagined seeing the shape or if he was simply going insane. He didn't completely understand what the word "insane" meant, but he had heard it enough in reference to his Grandpa to know that it connoted something troubling, something not quite right. While he refused to believe that there had ever been anything wrong about the old man, he instinctively understood that if there was anything wrong or aberrant about the images he was seeing, there might be no hope at all of being saved. Determined not to be disappointed again, he told himself that he would chase the shapes only after the sun came up -- once he could see in the clear light whether the shapes were real or the product of an insane mind -- but not before then, not until there was light. 'But why doesn't the light return?' he asked himself desperately?

But despite his determination to ignore the shapes, the next time one appeared he considered the possibility that the shape was indeed a dolphin and that what he was seeing was not a dolphin in isolation but the edge of the group, members on the periphery, all of whom were swimming parallel to him. In fact, they could have been only a few hundred yards to his left, he reasoned, and the dense darkness would have been enough to hide their presence from him and account for the now-you-see it/now-you-don't appearance and reappearance of the shapes. If this were the case, then it would be extremely unlikely that he would ever connect with them if he continued to veer toward shapes that were long gone by the time he arrived where he thought they were. One of the more interesting and troubling aspects of dolphin life was that despite appearances, they rarely traveled in a straight line. They moved up and down, back and forth, going from point A to point B effectively, albeit circuitously. This, and the possibility that he, too, was swimming just as erratically, potentially compounded his difficulty in finding them.

However, even if this was a more or less an accurate description of the situation, it still wasn't enough to guarantee that any changes he made in his efforts to find them would be fruitful. While he might be swimming parallel to them, he might also at the same time be swimming behind them, in which case every time he turned toward a shape, he might actually be wasting time and falling farther behind them and wasting precious energy that he could need later on. On the other hand...but he longed for paper and pencils to plot all this out. He longed for something human to take him out of this watery, bleak world.

Breaching the surface for a breath of air and then slipping back into the black water, he continued onward, fearing to move anywhere that might hurt his chances at finding them.

XIX

He was tired and hungry. Despite the rejuvenating breaths of air he forced himself to take from time to time, he could feel his strength fade. This was perhaps understandable, given the furious pace he had set, but it was also demoralizing because he feared that it was putting him father and farther behind the others. Despite the possibility of being in proximity, he increasingly feared that he was falling behind them and that he wouldn't reach safe waters in time for them to come to his aid.

Sooner or later, he would have to eat. He hadn't eaten in…well, he didn't want to consider how long, because he instinctively knew that this too would be demoralizing and weigh on his ability to keep moving. Clearly, he had to eat – he couldn't keep up his pace without some food -- but he told himself that he had enough energy left in him to wait to sunlight (if it ever came), after which he would feast, having found the others or not. Realistically, there was simply no way that a dolphin could hope to find food without at least one spec of light, and the bleak phosphorescence flashes below were too short and too dim to serve any practical use, and so what else was there to do but hope for the lights to come back as soon as possible?

It was hard, though, to resist the temptation to give up. He didn't want to quit now and allow the others to move on without him, but there were brief moments when he was particularly short of breath or when his hunger seemed particularly gnawing that he felt like stopping and…just stopping. He didn't know what would happen after he stopped and, in those brief moments when the feeling came over him, he didn't care. He didn't care about anything then, not the others, not himself, and not his mom or Bob. He still cared about his Grandpa, but he no longer mattered and would never again matter. It was strange that in those instances when he remembered his Grandpa, he could still discern the outline of his face, the color of his eyes, and the shaking of his jowls as he smiled. He could see the old man as if he were standing in front of him, alive and not dead. He could even feel his touch, which was always gentle despite the rough appearance of his old hands, and how frequently held him by the shoulders as if he were about to fall. And he remembered Grandpa telling him not to give up. "Don't be a quitter," he advised him. "No matter how bad things are, there will always be something better ahead. I promise you that."

He had almost come to believe that the old man was wrong and that better times would never again arise when he finally realized that he was going about finding the others in the stupidest of ways. The way he was going – swimming this way and that, hoping to find them in the nearest shallow water, chasing shapes that were probably phantoms of his imagination – was pointless and would only enable him to join the others by sheer luck. Even if they were nearby, the odds that he could intersect with them at this point in time were slim to none. No, he was wasting his time and risking his life. The only way (or at least the best way) to locate the others was to swim to a spot where they regularly visited, and wait for them. Sooner or later they would arrive. It was simple; it was so simple that he was surprised it hadn't occurred to him from the start. He sighed when he thought about all the time and energy he wasted for nothing. Well, there was a spot not far from where he was (if he was more or less correct about his location) where he could wait for them, a place that was in shallow waters, free from predators and replete with food. Of course, finding this location would be difficult despite its proximity. Of course, locating anything in darkness could be difficult, but he thought that he might be able to locate the reef by using the currents that he could feel rolling across his skin. The reef, if he remembered correctly, was located at the outermost edge of these same currents, just as they turned and flowed back toward the deep waters, and if he followed these currents they might lead him to the very place he sought. Naturally, finding the place didn't mean that they would be there, but since they visited the same places many times throughout a year, or as long as the food sources held out, there was every reason to expect them to show up eventually. In the meantime, he could fill his own aching belly and relax in safety. In fact, as he considered it, the amount of food available would provide a clue as to how soon they would arrive, for a lot of food would mean that they hadn't been there in a while and would therefore soon return. He smiled at this solution and wondered why he hadn't thought of it earlier.

Buoyed by this reasoning, he breached the surface with his head and sucked in the cool, night air. It no longer mattered if there was a moon or not, since he could feel the currents that would bring him to safety swirling around him – and he was increasingly confident that his inexplicable odyssey would soon come to an end.

The air, however, was strangely cold. The air often cooled down at night, but this time it seemed unusually brisk, and with each breath of air he could feel his lungs crackle, as if he was somewhere in the Arctic. This wasn't an entirely unpleasant sensation, for it sent shivers up and down his body that enlivened his other senses and made him feel (momentarily, at least) that he could follow the current effectively. Of course, it also intensified the gnawing pain in his stomach, but he was confident that he could hold out until he reached the reef. Taking one last gulp of cold, arctic air, and scanning the featureless, black night, he slipped beneath the surface and began following the current.

XX

Surprisingly, the current proved to be unsettling, inconsistent, and demanding. When he was in the center of it, he could feel it grasp his body with what seemed like stiff, icy fingers that pulled him this way and that, leading him to what he was beginning to view as his last stop, his home away from home, his refuge from everything that he was presently experiencing. But then there were other times when the current would unexpectedly release its grip on him, disappear, and reappear in some other place, often where he least expected to find it. It was at such moments that he felt as though he was losing home again, even if it really wasn't home but only a stop on a homeward journey.

Locating the current after losing it was troublesome because he was surrounded by other currents, each of which seemed to be vying for his attention, and he was frequently forced to break away from the current to surface for air, which then necessitated another search for the current that may or may not be in the same location where had last connected with it. This nerve-racking pattern of finding and losing the current, and finding it again, continued for some time until something inexplicable began to happen – the current seemed to be demanding that he move quicker, while his ability to respond to this demand was correspondingly weakening. The speed of the current had unexpectedly increased, but as it tried to pull him onward he could feel himself slipping from its grasp and he was afraid that he could lose all contact with it if he didn't push himself harder. Straining with every ounce of his being, he caught back up with the fingers and for a time continued their demanding pace, only to slow because this pace was too great and his strength was beginning to ebb. Every movement of his tail, each upward and downward thrust, was becoming increasingly difficult, and there was a brief moment when he thought that he would have to pause, allow the current to go on without him, before he could move another inch.

He didn't pause or break significantly from the current, though, because he didn't want to lose what he had gained and, he was certain, he was getting closer to his final destination. Or at least he told himself that he was getting closer. There were no visual signs or markers to measure the distance he had traveled, or that he was actually getting closer to anything – the moon, after all, was still black, and the sun had not begun to differentiate the water from the sky – and yet he told himself that it was only a matter of time before he reached his destination (as his mother might have said, he would be there before he knew it). Indeed, he told himself this over and over, and he also noted that it would only be a matter of minutes before there was something – smells, debris, the sounds of birds – that indicated he was nearing the reef. Naturally, there were still moments when his confidence flagged, when the absence of visual markers made him feel like he was standing still, and he would begin to doubt whether he would ever go home again. He wouldn't actually give up, although he would begin questioning if he was really doing right thing, going the correct way, or if he would ever be saved. Sometimes, when the water seemed colder and his shivering intensified, these doubts would become more frequent and persistent, and there were moments when his shivering was such that he couldn't tell if the fingers were still pulling him toward the reef or if the shaking movements of his body were deceiving him. But just when his doubts were at their worst, the most violent movements of his body would calm down and he would, once again, resume pushing himself with all his strength. Still, nothing came as easily to him as it did to the others. While he persevered, his strength slipped away, and even the most natural movements of his tail and body were difficult and forced; and there were moments when he was certain that he couldn't swim another inch without first stopping and sleeping to regain his energy. Thankfully, these moments were fairly rare, although his weakening condition forced him to breathe with increasing frequency, and he sometimes broke away from the current to check the surface for signs of the others or for the presence of predators.

Unlike his previous, ebullient efforts to break the surface of the water, he would now carefully push his head through the surface of the water so that nothing would interfere with his ability to hear the presence of anything around him. Although seeing anything in the impenetrable darkness was practically impossible, the night intensified his hearing, and because it did the same with all the creatures of the night, he was careful not to make the slightest sound as he turned to focus his ears in every direction. But no matter how many times he pivoted, straining his ears and even sense of smell, there never seemed to be anything, not even a vibration emanating from a single drop of water. Each time he was confronted with the silence, he was disappointed, because it suggested that the others were not close enough to make their presence known; but, on the other hand, it also suggested that no one else was close by either, such as one of the horrible creatures from the depths below him. By itself, this should have been enough to put his mind at ease, but he couldn't help wondering if his shivering was sending out unseen signals to those creatures, who might even now be waiting for the opportunity to strike. If he had learned one thing about predators, it was that the victims were more often than not unaware of the predator's presence until the first strike, which meant that the end cam come swiftly no matter what precautions were taken. Lately, however, while he tried to be as quiet as a mouse when he took a long draft of icy-cold air, he was beginning to feel increasingly uneasy, wondering if he was missing something, if he had failed to do something to ensure his survival. But as he invariably turned around one more time, straining his ears to determine if there was anything nearby that had occasioned his nervousness, he found only silence, absolute silence, after which he would quietly slip back between the surface and continue on, steadily and sometimes painfully pushing his tail up and down.

He was determined to reach the reef as quickly as he could, albeit with a controlled, mechanical rhythm to his movements so that predators would not mistake him for an animal in distress (the favorite mark of any predator). But he was not always able to balance speed with unvarying movement, because he was often forced to pause, turn, and twist his body to make sure he was following the right current. And it was sometimes the case that he was shaking so badly that he couldn't distinguish the movements of his body from the tendrils of the current, and he would nearly come to a complete halt to assure himself that the fingers were still caressing his skin and that he was indeed swimming in the correct direction. The presence of the fingers, their ability to encompass his entire body and pull him forward, renewed his sense of purpose and increased his determination to reach the reef, even if it did little to increase his strength or prevent him from gradually losing speed.

Despite his troubles, his mind remained clear – neither the cold water nor his nearly exhausted physical state clouded his mental functions, even if his body was increasingly resistant to his mind's commands – and, in a way, he was beginning to feel like he had just awoken from a profound nap and had to bring all his mental energies to bear on even the simplest of problems, such as where he was going and his purpose in going there. Sometimes, when he needed to concentrate on moving forward, he would instead dream about being a human and recall some of the best moments of his childhood. One time, as the struggle to move was particularly hard and his lungs ached from the lack of oxygen, he recalled his home, which was special because his mother lived there and, among other things, it housed the family's photographs, which were distributed around the house and included shots of himself, his mother, Bob, and of course Grandpa. There were a lot of photographs of his Grandpa throughout the house – in a tuxedo at the wedding of a young, handsome, and smiling couple, and flanked by the same couple, only years later, holding a baby, covered in soft, light-blue blankets between which only his nose and chin poked out – and many more in his own bedroom, covering the back wall behind the headboard of his bed. These were exotic images – shots taken while the old man was on some magical journey (on the plains of Africa, in front of the Great Wall of China, at the base of the Sphinx, leaning against a Redwood tree in California, and on and on) – none of which, strangely, showed him anywhere near water, unless he was drinking from the fountains in a heavily forested city garden during what was called a Bavarian Oktoberfest. His Grandpa loved the ocean and had spoken about it so many times, and yet he couldn't remember a single picture of the old man anywhere near a great body of water. It was sad, because he knew how much his Grandpa loved the water and now had no way of connecting him to the ocean except through his own memories. There were even pictures of his mother at some beach (long before he had become a reality), although she had never spoken of her time there. Remembering his mother, who always seemed flustered, and Bob, who always seemed distant, troubled him and made him regret not leaving a note or informing them where he was going. 'Were they sad?' he wondered.

He might have continued on in this vein, but the very instant he saw his mother weeping in his absence, something slammed into his side, back near the very end of his body, sending him spinning into the opposite direction. For a moment or two, he was dazed and didn't have the slightest idea what had happened, but as he regained his senses he realized that he had either run into something or something had run into him. He looked carefully in the direction of the blow, but he could see little but the interminable blackness of the water and the occasional phosphorescence from the abyss below.

Despite the force of the blow, he didn't seem to be hurt, at least not seriously. He could feel a slight discomfort on his back where he was hit, but everything else felt normal, unharmed. Shortly after this his tail began to be numb, which was probably to be expected given the force of the blow. But what had happened? Had something run into him and, if so, what was it and where was it? It had to have been large, since the impact traveled throughout his entire body, and he could still feel the speed with which his body whipped around. What had the strength to deliver such a blow? He wasn't certain that he wanted the answer, and yet he couldn't stop rolling the question around in his mind, toying with it, considering a myriad of possibilities, none of which made the prospect of going home more assured. Strangely, his shaking stopped, and he easily located the current; he also seemed to pick up speed as he followed it, as if nothing had happened.

XXI

He was able to follow the current for some time, swimming in the center of it and feeling its fingers pull his skin. There were some instances in which the pull became slightly painful, particularly in the area of his body that had been hit, but the pain hadn't been unbearable and, for the most part, it had affected him only intermittently. More importantly, he was able to follow the current even when he was forced to the surface for air, which seemed to be happening more and more frequently. For some reason, he seemed unable to hold his breath for any reasonable amount of time, and he could tell when he needed air not because his lungs began to hurt but because he began to get lightheaded. He was certain that it didn't mean anything, although it was a nuisance, and in this state instead of pushing himself to the surface with several strong pushes from his tail, he tended to float to the surface, pushing his body with a couple of weak thrusts and letting nature take care of itself after that.

After he reached the surface, he would quietly take several deep breaths of air and hold his breath as he pirouetted several times listening for something other than his own movement in the water. Once, he thought he heard a familiar slap on the surface of the water, but the sound was so faint that he couldn't decide whether he had actually heard a slap or was deceived by his imagination, which may have responded to an especially loud thump from his heart. But since he was never able to identify the cause of the sound, he was eventually forced to concede that it was most likely the product of his overwrought imagination, a dispiriting conclusion that made it harder for him to continue moving, especially now that his strength was decreasing and the discomfort in his tail was increasing. More than anything else at that moment, he needed something that would give him hope that he was headed in the right direction and that he would shortly be reunited with those he loved. 'If only Grandpa were with me,' he thought. 'He would know what to do. He would be able to explain the unending night. He would talk to me, pet me, and make everything better.' When he was a boy, he knew that whenever he was afraid, whenever he had questions, whenever he needed answers, he could always call his Grandpa (when he wasn't visiting) or run to him and hold him tightly around the waist (when he was), and the old man would settle his mind and heart, providing the love and support that he needed now more than anything else, more than air itself. But his Grandpa was gone, and he didn't have anyone else he could turn to, and so he was forced to find his own way out of this predicament.

This time when he surfaced, he turned around several times, each time more slowly than the last. Exposing only the top of his head, he strained his hearing for anything which might indicate that he was close to the reef, to the others, or...or to something. There was nothing; even when he shook his head slightly, there was no response from the motionless water, nothing that disturbed the deathly stillness surrounding him. Suddenly resolved to risk alerting predators, he began clicking and squeaking to see if anyone could hear him or, if not, to see if the sound waves from his clicking returned, which would indicate a solid object nearby, perhaps land or proof that he was close to the reef. But again there was nothing, no returned clicks, no echoes, no anything that would suggest that he wasn't floating over a vast, bottomless pit of water, the dimensions of which were as unfathomable as its depth. As he had done previously, he sniffed the air for any signs of life or nearby land, which could be easily be detected miles from the shore. Nothing. Determined to persevere, he took one more breath and this time, instead of dropping beneath the surface and searching for the current, he kept his head, back, and tail on the surface of the water and began to move slowly forward, slapping his tail rhythmically against the surface to let the others know where he was, and to relieve the increasingly unbearable quietness. But even this produced nothing – nothing, nothing, nothing, except a response from his heart, which was beginning to resonate uncomfortably throughout his body.

A few minutes later, he was suddenly seized with the desire to scream at the top of his lungs – not to seek the others, but to end the dull silence that was closing in on him and threatening his...sanity. Once again, there was no better word for what he was feeling. Somehow, however, he was able to resist the urge, and, after taking a deep breath, he felt able to control himself again – and he need to control himself not simply to justify his smile, but also to prevent the fear of the unknown or the barely understood from overwhelming him and destroying him. He knew that any signs of weakness or disorientation would make him a tantalizing target for the monsters from the depths below him, and so he told himself that despite his momentary desire to destroy the silence, he had not yet done anything that would awaken the interest of those beings swimming somewhere beneath him. Finding a reserve of determination, he promised himself that he would survive the night, and once the warm, reassuring light from the sun arrived, he would find the others and ensure that such predicaments never again happened to him. 'If only the sun would rise,' he added, because the sun alone seemed to have the power to loosen his stiffening body and ease the irrational terrors of the darkness that swirled around him. But while the thought of the sun's brilliant gold and yellow rays spreading across the shimmering surface of the water helped ease his fears, it did nothing to lessen the increasing discomfort that was engulfing his tail, making it difficult if not impossible to believe that it was little more than a freak of his imagination. In fact, the pain was increasing at an astonishing rate, twisting his insides and coursing up and down his back like nothing he had ever experienced before, and he was no longer able to dismiss the injury as inconsequential or a minor impact caused by hitting a piece of coral. (On the other hand, it wasn't caused by a propeller, because that would have killed him outright.) He was now forced to accept the fact that he was injured, perhaps seriously.

'It hurts,' he squeaked to himself, 'but I can handle it, and when the sun comes up I can see what happened.'

Dropping beneath the surface, he located the current (actually, the current located him), and he began to follow it. He moved slowly and rhythmically, keeping his movements to a minimum to protect himself from predators and, at the same time, to conserve his energy. He felt certain that at this pace, he could keep going for quite a while without stopping and resting. While this was possibly true, it was also the case that the pain in his tail was increasing with every movement – sometimes, it felt like someone was stabbing him in the back, while at other times the

ROB G. LERNER

pain had no specific location and simply ran up and down his tail and back
– and there were moments in which his lower body seemed to resist all
effort to move at any other pace. He longed for the light, any light, to
guide his way and reveal some place where he could warm his body and
fill his stomach with the first real food that he had had in quite some time.

XXII

He moved onward throughout the endless night, riding the current like a surfer to conserve his energy and ease the discomfort in his tail and back. There were moments when he could hear the beating of his heart, which felt like someone pounding inside his chest, but the noise would subside, and he would surface and listen intently for something other than his heart beat. But like every other time he tried to locate something above or below the surface, the result was nothing; there was no sound anywhere, not on the surface of the water or beneath it, and absolutely nothing that would suggest the presence of life. In fact, it had been so long since he had heard a sound outside himself that the silence was beginning to seem normal, just as the shouts and screams of little children seem normal in another environment.

Still, the silence kept him on edge, forcing him to keep a wary, if unseeing, eye out for anything that might be dangerous. Once again, the only lights so far that had penetrated the thick darkness which surrounded him were the brief phosphorescent flashes that flared and sparkled from the inaccessible depths below. These were so brief that he often wondered if he had seen them at all, half believing that his blind eyes were playing tricks on him, like they did when he flicked the lights on and off in his bedroom at night, creating afterimages that would pulsate briefly before fading into nothingness. Unfortunately, these weren't afterimages, and he couldn't help wondering if they were harbingers of something terrible, especially when the flashes would fly up almost within reach before falling backwards and merging with the blackness. Had it come for him?

Tearing himself away from the flashes, he turned his blind eyes forward in the direction of the current and, as he did so, he spotted a faint pinkish light in the distance to his right. It really wasn't much of a light (it was hardly more than a short, horizontal smudge); it wasn't bright enough for any practical purpose; and yet because it was the first seemingly benign light that he had observed since the moon disappeared, it lifted his spirits

91

and filled him with a hope that the sun (or moon) might soon be inching up over the horizon. But as he strained his eyes to determine the origin of the light, it became clear that it wasn't caused by either the sun or the moon (unlike sunlight, this was a narrow smudge of color that occupied only one small area in the distance) but had some other origin. It certainly didn't bear a resemblance to the phosphorescent flashes below, which had a different color and were even more diffused, not to mention coming from a direction the polar opposite of which the pink haze originated; and unlike the flashes from below, the pink light glowed steadily, becoming neither lighter nor darker regardless of how long he starred at it. Although he realized that changing directions now could have life and death consequences, he couldn't resist the temptation to turn away from the current and investigate the pink light, even if swimming toward it could exhaust what little strength he had left.

He tried not to think about the risk, or his ebbing strength or the pain, or the fact that his body was becoming increasingly stiff, as if he were in the grip of an invisible giant whose grasp prevented his body from moving in any but the most rudimentary ways. But as he moved on, with greater and greater difficulty, the pounding in his chest returning and reverberating throughout his body, he suddenly caught sight of something near the light, something that seemed to move in front of the light, momentarily darkening a portion of it so that he could see what appeared to be shadow. This time, it didn't try to hide in the periphery of his vision, as if it were trying to instill confusion and doubt in his mind; while he couldn't identify its shadow (it was elongated, although he was too far away to make out enough details to say whether this elongation was a fish or a person or even a tree), he was certain that it was not his imagination and that it was alive, since it clearly moved while the light itself remained fixed. Blinking several times to clear his vision and to make sure his senses were alert, he noticed shortly after the first sighting another shadow crossing the light and, shortly after this, two shadows moving in tandem, this time reaching down instead of across the light. Could it be the others? It was impossible to tell at that moment, but the possibility infused him with a small amount of additional energy that he knew was enough to carry him to the exact location.

XXIII

He began with a much quicker pace than he had had for some time. Unfortunately, it was to last only a few minutes before he slowed down to his previous pace and then, if that were possible, slowed some more until he was hardly moving. It was impossible to move any faster, not until his strength came back and the pain dissipated a little (on the contrary, it was increasing with each movement he was still able to produce). The light held steady, though, even though he never seemed to get any closer to it, as if it had a mind of its own and was refusing to allow him to reach it. But at least it was something, something that offset the unending blackness that was beginning to seem without end. Like a marathon runner, he refused to give up, not until he reached the light and the shadows crossing it; indeed, there was no point in going back, since he probably lacked the strength to follow the current again and, realistically, it would be difficult to find the current again – he could no longer remember where it was or in which direction it had been moving.

Unlike the previous times he had seen a shadow or a shape, he remained steadfast in his conviction that he had seen something and that this something was not a figment of his imagination. He didn't know what this something was, or exactly where it was (if it wasn't actually crossing the light), but he was never more certain of anything in his life that it was something animate. He hoped that it was one of the others, and, if this were so, it was likely that not one but many somethings had crossed the light (certainly, this was the case with the two shadows that came down from the surface). It made sense, because dolphins rarely paced back and forth like dumb sharks; they were constantly moving in every direction, even when they appeared to be swimming and leaping in unison (it was their nature to be curious, and it was impossible to satisfy one's curiosity while lumbering in a straight line like an overloaded, hungry truck). The shadows therefore had to be dolphins, he told himself, as he saw another one of the shadows cross the light. This one was also indistinct, and its movement from right to left seemed less curious than methodical, but it

93

had to be the others – it had to be the others, because there was nothing else around.

'But if it's not one of the others,' he wondered in a vague way, which animals will sometimes do when gravely wounded, 'then what is it?' He didn't stop to ponder the question or its possibilities but kept moving, slowly and automatically, as if he was no longer in control of his body but went wherever it directed him.

The light remained steady and the shadows or objects now and again moved across it, momentarily blocking it out and leaving him in complete darkness, after which the light would again shine as it did before.

After a while, he again asked himself the question. 'What is it? I know there something there, and if it's not one of the others, what could it be? Could it be my reflection on the black water?' He didn't know how this could happen, unless perhaps a flash of phosphorescence from below cast his image in the black wall in front of him. It was certainly possible, although he didn't understand the physics that would have made that possible – or impossible. Of course, to admit this possibility was also to accept the fact that he was heading farther and farther away from the current and every possibility of finding the reef – and without the reef's shallow waters, he had no way of protecting himself, feeding, or finding the others. For now, however, he dropped this possibility.

Two more times he caught sight of the elusive shape, and each time like the last – and how many times had it been? – he was left with the burning question of what it was and the hope that it was indeed one of the others.

More than ever, he was ready to go home, and more than anything else he wanted to see his Grandpa. He couldn't quite believe that the old man was gone. It didn't make sense. He needed his Grandpa, because he was the only one who could have explained the shapes, who would have helped him out of this agonizing predicament, and the old man would have held him, kissed him, and whispered endearments into his ears. Even if he stumbled on the others now, none of them could have provided any of this, none of them could have provided anything other than the same frozen smiles that they offered everyone, everything, and every time. But if his Grandpa wasn't available, he would have gladly settled for his mom and Bob, even if that meant he would be in trouble for his all too numerous transgressions. He wanted to go home; he wanted to go to his room, to visit his friends, to see his mother. He missed everyone and knew now that it had all been a big mistake.

'Maybe,' he told himself, as he reflected on both his predicament and his life with the others, 'Maybe I can do things differently. Maybe if I…'

As he began to consider these things, both this world and the one he left behind, he noticed that one of the shadows was directly in front of him, perhaps two or three hundred yards away. Or at least he thought it was. He couldn't tell for sure, since it was as indistinct as all the others, although something reassured him that it was closer than the other shadows, almost at hand, even if there was nothing to measure its proximity other than the amount of time (measured in seconds) that it blotted out the light. Clearly, something was there, even if it wasn't as close as it seemed, and its presence was both exciting and frustrating – frustrating because he still couldn't discern what it was. It was probably one of the others, although it could simply be another fish in the ocean (possibly a big, ugly grouper, which was annoying because it was so ugly)…or simply something else entirely. But as he continued to get closer, inching along at a pace that seemed barely faster than standing still, he was beginning to see something beyond the light, as if the shadow no longer had to cross the light in order to be outlined, although this outline still wasn't clear enough in the darkness to answer the question – 'Is it one of the others?' One of the reasons that the shadow was not completely identifiable was the inexplicable and silent turbulence in the water, which blurred the shadow (or shadows, because he still refused to accept that there was just one) and made tracking it difficult (he was beginning to bounce up and down in its wake).

The turbulence, however, may have been just what he needed. While it clouded his vision and jarred his insides (the pain seemed to be reaching deeper into his body), it quickly filled him with the same kind of hope that the current once did – that is, he might be able to follow it to the shapes – or the others, if indeed they were the shapes. In fact, he might be able to ride it to them – the turbulence was at times wave-like in its violence and proportions – which would conserve his badly needed energy, lessen the strain he was placing on his injuries, and increase the speed to his eventual reunion.

Filled with a new sense of purpose, his strength increased momentarily (not enough to dissipate the pain, however) and he pushed himself to the surface, where he filled his lungs with delicious, energizing air. He was almost certain that the end of his troubles was at hand.

XXIV

Indeed, the sky seemed to be pushing the black night back, and he could see some vague hints that the sun might rise in an hour or so. He looked down at the water and, even though it was still bleak and impenetrable, he was positive that he could discern the difference between the surface and the water below, in addition to noticing some slight variations in the water beneath him, as if the turbulence could now be detected visually as well as tactilely.

Slipping back beneath the surface, he began gliding downward toward the turbulence, determined to find the others or, at the very least, identify the shapes. Unlike his previous excitement, he was ebullient and filled with the certainty that his travails would soon end and that he would find the others, if he hadn't already found them in the shadows. In fact, the hint of sunlight and the promise that the sun would finally rise (a promise that he made to himself) not only excited him but also reenergized him to an extraordinary degree, giving him a strength that he had begun to accept was lost forever. He was now confident that he could last until sunrise, and he was certain that he could hold out until he reached the reef, no matter how many miles he had to swim (he knew the reef was close by, otherwise the presence of so many shadows didn't make sense). As he continued to pick up speed, he couldn't help thinking about ways of persuading the others to return to the beach where he left land (he didn't want to launch off by himself, especially because he no longer remembered where the beach was and certainly didn't want to experience another night by himself) and what he would do if by chance he spotted his mom or Bob. 'What if Grandpa was there,' he asked himself. 'Is it possible?' The possibility of achieving the impossible pushed him forward and, despite the ever-present pain, he moved as hard and as fast as he could.

His downward path was smooth and quick, and within seconds he was coming to the edge of the turbulence. But just as he was about to leap into the churning water, he suddenly stopped and abruptly began accelerating in the opposite direction, as if something had grabbed him from behind and was pulling him backwards, away from the shadows and down toward the abyss. The rate of his acceleration was blinding, and the force holding onto his body was unrelenting – it felt like he had been grabbed by a giant hand that was intent on dragging him back into the darkness and forcing all the air out of his lungs, which swarmed around him in a haze of reddish bubbles. But just as suddenly as the unseen force had grabbed him, it released him, allowing him to regain his senses and the movement of his body.

For a few moments, he felt neither pain nor fear, and instinctively he tried to straighten himself out and rush to the surface, where he could savor the very air that only moments ago he was certain he wouldn't need for some time. Certain that he was free from the unseen hand – and, at the same time, in complete control of his senses and body – he tried to move but was suddenly blinded by a rush of bubbles that engulfed not only his body but seemingly everything around him. Although the light was steadily increasing ('The sun must be rising,' he told himself), he could see nothing but a mesh of furiously bouncing bubbles, clouding his senses (which way was up?) and suddenly filling him with a fear, the intensity of which he had not experienced in this world or the other.

He struggled to move out of the bubbles. Even though the bubbles signified the life-giving air that he now needed desperately, he also realized instinctively that the bubbles also represented something inexpressibly dire, something from which he had only seconds to escape. But every movement he made seemed slow and not nearly fast enough to push him to safety; and every movement was now also fraught with intense pain unlike anything he had yet experienced. At first, slender rills of pain shot throughout his body, beginning somewhere behind him and coursing up through his head. Then these slender rills suddenly changed into a raging fire that seemed to engulf nearly every inch of him, from head to foot; even his face, which had neither seen nor felt the source of the impact, seemed on fire and felt ready to burst. Nonetheless, he kept pushing himself, giving no thought to preserving his energy or angling in any particular direction – any direction at this point was acceptable.

Before he could recover and move outside of the hideous bubbles, which no doubt reflected great harm, he was quickly buffeted by a series of sharp, stinging blows to the stomach, which forced the remaining air out of his lungs and sapped whatever strength he had left. The blows didn't stop, however, and, unable to move or defend himself, he could feel his body float in one direction and then another from the force of the blows. He needed air desperately, although he lacked the ability to fight for it, or even reach out for the surface, as if that were somewhere close by.

The blows ceased as abruptly as they had begun, and he floated downward past the bubbles and currents until he reached the bottom and rested gently on his side, his left eye staring up at the dim, evanescent light far overhead. The sensation of falling helplessly, unable to do anything to control his movement, reminded him of the toy boats that he forced under the soapy surface of his bath water – once they hit the bottom of the tub, they would roll over on their side and rock back and forth, moved this way and that by the unseen currents beneath the surface. He had always been fascinated by these hapless boats – by their inability to do anything but to submit to the unseen forces under the water – and he had often wondered what it would be like moving only where the currents moved him, safe from all the vicissitudes overhead. To tell the truth, his current state was not in the least unpleasant. In fact, it felt restful, and what he needed now was rest, plenty of rest.

'I wonder what they're doing?' he asked himself, while staring blankly into the abyss. 'I wonder where they are and if they know I'm missing?' He might have cried, feeling sorry for himself, but at the moment he felt no sorrow, or pity, or any other emotion. His heart was as dull as the ocean around him, and so his exclamations were merely ruminations, devoid of concern for either the others or himself. He saw nothing, thought nothing, for some time afterward until another thought sprang up in his consciousness. 'They live wonderful lives,' he continued, suddenly feeling that he had seen the last of them, that he would never be reunited with them, although he didn't know why this should be so despite his present situation. Still, he wasn't sad, maybe pensive, but at least not distraught over his situation. He didn't think about his situation; for some reason, it didn't exist for him.

'Why do dolphins always smile?' he asked himself, genuinely curious about the great mammals. 'They are surrounded by danger all the time, and yet they always smile, even when danger forces them to move from one place to another in a hurry. They rarely do fun things, but they are always happy. Yes, there is all the swimming and jumping and sounding, but what happens after that, and is 'what happens' interesting and satisfying enough to make them smile day and night? It doesn't make sense, especially when the relationships are not special, or are not special enough to have friends and connections that cannot be shared by anyone else.' He thought about one of the larger dolphins, the one which had disappeared with the ball of fish, and he recalled how much he liked him, although he couldn't exactly recall why he liked him or what set him apart from the others, unless it was his size and the scars -- long, gray, and jagged striations – that ran down his back and left side. The scars suggested that he had experienced some difficult times, and yet he had clearly been able to put those times behind him so that he could get the best out of his life, whatever that meant to him. But as he thought about it, as he remembered the dolphin's scars and his smiling face every time he looked at him, he began to think that it was this -- getting past the adversity and making the most out of life – that made him interesting, this and the fact the he was friendly and smiling and protective.

This is what his Grandpa was like, except that he showered him with more affection than he did anyone else, especially his mom, with whom he always seemed to be arguing. The arguments were strange and didn't make sense. He seemed to be at the center of most of them (and, in fact, seemed to be present at lot of them), his Grandpa defending him, while his mom…well, he couldn't remember what made her so angry.

'You were supposed to be watching him," he remembered his mom saying, speaking to the old man as if he were a child and, at the same time, clearly trying to control her emotions. She was standing directly in front of Grandpa, her arms folded across her breast, and her lips and jaw set tightly. It was dark and rainy outside, and she must have just come in from outside, because her hair was visibly wet and she was wearing a jacket that was soaked, especially on the shoulders.

"He's okay," Grandpa replied, as he sat in a comfortable chair in the living room. Unlike his mom, he was completely dry and was wearing some of his favorite indoor clothes (a brown corduroy sport coat, baggy green corduroy pants, and his beat up slippers), which he only rarely changed. He seemed calm and relaxed, and his main concern lay in the fact that his mom had turned off the TV before she began to speak. "It was an accident, and so you've told him not to go out without telling you, and that's that. What more do you need to say? Now, if you don't mind..."

"What? You make it sound like it was his fault. I asked you to watch him while I went out, and when I come back he's gone, you're asleep in front of the TV, and you don't have a clue what's happened."

"I don't understand why you're so upset. Is he okay? I'm sure he is. Now, what more do we need to say about...I've forgotten. But it doesn't matter. If there's trouble, you've got...what was his name again?"

"Bob," she replied slowly, as if his failure to remember Bob's name was as great a sin, albeit it of a different kind. "Bob, but Bob isn't here because he's out of town on business. I needed you for ten minutes while I...but you couldn't even do this. Not ten simple minutes. Do you known where he was?"

"Bob?"

"No, you old fool," his mom screamed. "Try to get this through your head. When I came home and he wasn't with you, I went looking for him. I don't know why, but I went to the lake, thinking that he might be there at the edge of the water, like he does some times when he's not supposed to." She glanced at him before turning back to the old man. "And I was lucky I did. That's where he was, but he was waist deep in the water."

"Okay," he responded, nodding his head as if he understood her.

"No, it's not okay. He can't swim, and to top it off the weather was like this. Can't you see what's happening outside?"

He strained his neck to see around her (there was a large window to her back, although the curtains had been pulled tightly together), but when he couldn't see anything from his vantage point he turned back to her, and looked up at her dour face. "I don't see anything. You're in the…"

"There's a storm outside, there's lightening, the sun is down, and the waves on the lake were high. If I hadn't been there just then, I don't know what might have happened." She paused momentarily to calm her nerves and to keep from crying. "He could have been…one of these times…don't you understand me? Don't you understand me, Papa? He could have been hurt. He could have been killed. You should have been watching him."

His Grandpa didn't appear to understand what she meant, but it was clear that he understood that he had done something wrong, although he wasn't certain what. For a few moments he stared up at her, his face reddening and his eyes welling up with tears. "Darling," he said, breaking the painful silence between them. "I don't know. He wasn't hurt, was he?"

"No," his mom said with an eerie finality.

"Then what's wrong? Why are you so angry with me?"

His mom paused. "I'm not." She turned to walk away, but he reached across and grabbed her arm lightly.

"Is everything okay," he asked as looked up at her and she looked down at him.

"Yes," she replied with a faint smile on her lips.

"Please, can I stay? They come into my room at that place, and they take my things. I...I don't know what to do..."

She pulled his hand off her arm and, sniffing a couple of times to keep her tears back, she shook her head. "Right now I have enough trouble watching over..." She couldn't finish her statement.

After she had left the room, he walked over to his Grandpa and put his arm around his shoulders. The old man was hunched over, and he could feel his shoulders shake. The old man sighed, shook his head, and then, without looking up, reached around and held him by his waist. Turning toward him, forcing a smile on his old, weathered face, he said, "You listen to me. I will never leave you. You can always count on me. Your mother...all she cares about is that man, what's his name. You be careful, or she will throw you away, too. It's always about that man." He pulled the boy close to him, kissed him on the top of his head, and then let him go. "Why are you so wet?" he added, genuinely perplexed by the boy's wet clothes. "Well, never mind. Bring me the remote, sweetie. Let's find the ocean channel."

XXV

Timmy was hit with a blinding burst of golden light. He shut his eyes and instinctively covered them with his left hand. But instead of turning away from the light, he remained motionless and, spreading his fingers from time to time to let in increasingly larger amounts of diffuse light, waited until his eyes adjusted to the new conditions before removing his land and allowing his hand and arm to drop softly to his side. Opening his eyes normally (and blinking several times to ease the residual discomfort he still felt in the bright light), he was surprised to see that he was not at the bottom of the ocean but on narrow spit of sand only a few feet from the water. Moreover, as he regained his senses, he realized that he was lying on his back with a soft pillow of sand behind his head and facing the horizon.

The air was warm, and its smell reminded him of the aquarium that he and his Grandpa visited long ago. Timmy felt surprisingly comfortable lying in the soft sand and, recalling his experience in the frigid Arctic waters, he was in no hurry to move anywhere or do anything. His desire to stay put increased when he looked at the waves, which were visible between his feet and toes. Although large, the waves weren't close enough to force him to higher ground; and so he pushed the back of his head deeper in the sand and stared up at the sky, observing the frenzied movements of small birds and watching the clouds, which were moving rapidly from left to right and becoming increasingly darker. A storm was clearly approaching. By itself, this was no reason to scurry off the beach, but when the wind suddenly picked up and sent a chill throughout his body, he raised his head and examined the waves more closely. The storm was closer than he had imagined, and yet he was still confident that he had plenty of time before he needed to do anything in response. In the meantime, with his head raised, he idly scanned the surface of the water for signs of life and then glanced around to see if he recognized the area. The beach was deserted and, while he didn't see anything that looked especially familiar, a number of things were almost recognizable, such as the slope of the beach near the water and the manner in which the sand rolled off his skin (it reminded of grains of sand in an hourglass). There were other things, too, although every time he looked closely at them their familiarity immediately vanished (in one instance, a child's small footprints proved to be indentations in the sand caused by the action of waves). 'Maybe,' he told himself, 'I'm just not used to seeing things outside of the water.'

Timmy was still weak and tired, but at least he felt much better than he had only moments earlier when he felt incapable of responding to the dangers under the water. In fact, by comparison, he felt almost normal. There was no real pain, and though he didn't feel like extending himself, he could raise and lower his head and move his fingers and toes quite easily. He was hungry and this seemed like a good sign, because it suggested that whatever had happened earlier was having no residual effect on the normal functioning of his body. In fact, he had no reason to doubt his ability to move freely, although at the moment he didn't want to do anything except lie in the sand and stare at the sky.

XXVI

Timmy remained on his back for some time. He didn't worry about the approaching storm or concern himself with much of anything else. But after a while, the sights, sounds, and smells that surrounded him began to revive his spirits in a way that he couldn't have imagined was possible only moments ago. Adjusting himself slightly so that he could see the entire ocean from his perch in the sand, he again scanned its heaving blue surface for ocean life; at the same time, he marveled at the raucous chatter of the birds overhead and couldn't help inhaling over and over the salty ocean air, as if this was the first time he had ever tasted something so pleasant. He loved the ocean, he loved the caress of the water as it hissed across the sand and wrapped itself around his legs and sides, and he was amazed that the mere sight of the waves pounding at the edge of the sand evoked in him powerful emotions that he couldn't begin to comprehend. But the sand, too, the feeling of solidity and permanence, tugged at him emotionally, although he was certain that its appeal lay in the fact that he had found what he had been looking for and that there was nothing else that he had to do.

Relaxed, feeling safe and confident that he had finally escaped danger, he slowly became aware of bits and pieces of singing, or talking, or something. The sounds – barks, gurgles, and screeches – were for the most part gibberish, but there were moments when these odd sounds were almost intelligible, as if he were hearing bits and pieces of a conversation in which the speakers were too far away to understand but not so far away that their words weren't recognizable as language. For a few seconds he couldn't help training his ears on these sounds, but because he couldn't make sense of them – because he sometimes had trouble separating the sounds from all the other gibberish that filled the air – he told himself that the sounds were nothing, pointless, and that he was wasting his time trying to identify them. Adjusting his head in the sand, smoothing out the little lumps at the base of his skull that made his head sore, he was about to conclude that the sounds were probably the result of a tired, food-deprived

106

brain, a brain that used to transform thick, low-hanging clouds into courageous knights and fearsome dragons, he noticed that the sounds were getting louder and more insistent, at times completely drowning out the racket from the birds.

Timmy lifted up his head and scanned the horizon to locate the source of the sounds. He observed the sky, the water, and the crashing waves, which exploded after they curled inward and crashed onto the turbulent surface of the water, forcing the remnants onto the shore and toward his feet. But no sooner had he noticed the death throes of one particularly large wave than he began to notice that the barks, gurgles, and screeches were becoming softer and harder to distinguish from all the other noises surrounding him -- the pounding of the waves, the screeching of the birds, and the constant hiss from the water crossing the sand. The rapidly-changing volume surprised him and, although he was confident that his bodily strength was returning, he was beginning to wonder if his mind – equally tired from the strain of seeking home in the darkness – was recuperating at a much slower pace and unable to muster the inner reserves needed to understand the barks and distinguish them from every other sound or noise surrounding him. Timmy sighed in frustration and was about to rest his head on the sand when he caught sight of those unmistakable signs of dolphins – the gray fins on the arching backs of the animals as they cut through the air in search of food before slipping back beneath the opaque surface of the water. He found them! After all the days, months, and years that he had been searching for them, he had finally found them and could consider this strange, unnerving journey at an end. Oh, what an amazing sight, especially as the cacophony surrounding him began to coalesce into the beautiful music that the dolphins made as they communicated with one another – and with him. They were singing, and yet as he listened intently hoping to divine how long they would be staying in these waters and where they planned to go next, he was somewhat disconcerted that he couldn't understand a single note of their music. Of course, he had always had trouble deciphering the sounds they made, but it suddenly seemed that he was even less proficient than he had been when he first made contact with them. It didn't make sense, although maybe it didn't matter because he had found them at last.

No, it didn't matter whether he understood their music or not. Raising himself on his elbows and marveling at the beauty of their smooth skin and smiling, loving faces, he couldn't resist pulling and pushing himself toward the water, using only his elbows and the heels of his feet. Once he could feel the cool water flowing over the lower half of his body, he forced himself deeper into the water until he was neck deep in the water and bouncing on the balls of his feet to keep from going completely under the surface. Timmy was determined to see them clearly and perhaps touch them one more time, to caress their bodies in appreciation for all the love that they had provided him, after which he would...he smiled wistfully, because for some reason he didn't know what he would do next. He had come a long way to be reunited with them, but now that they were within his reach going back to his dolphin life didn't seem as important as it once did. And what was stranger still, he didn't seem to know what was more important, unless it was to see his Grandpa and spend the rest of his life with the old man. Moving slowly, not allowing the water reach beyond his head (he gauged the depth every now and then by touching the bottom with his left foot), he finally came to a spot where he could see them clearly without having to commit himself to the sea. Timmy didn't try to understand the reason behind his hesitation to take another step, even though he had gone this far with every intention to swim in their midst, to relive the love that they once showered on him. For the moment, he was content to keep his distance and watch their movements, as if this were enough to satisfy his desires for now. The dolphins kept their distance as well, as if they were unaware of his presence and determined to swim back and forth in search of invisible fish.

Smiling as hard as he could, blowing water out of his nose whenever he was hit by a small wave, Timmy was watching the dolphins intently, feeling their presence as clearly as he could see their sleek, silver shapes, when he noticed that the sun was no longer overhead, covering everything with a warm, golden glow, but was now hovering just above the horizon like an angry, red eye and casting its blood-red color across both the sky and the water. It didn't make sense – how could the sun have moved so quickly that he hadn't noticed its progression? Or observed the alteration in its color? What's more, as he looked around trying to make sense of the changes, he also noticed near the beach on his left several old, Victorian houses and on his right huge sand dunes that seemed to isolate this section of the beach. He reassured himself that he had never seen either the houses or dunes before, but he suddenly began to feel as if he had been transported back to the time and place when he first met the dolphins. Timmy couldn't explain this disquieting sensation; he told himself that there was no proof that today was yesterday and not today; and yet he couldn't help feeling that everything that had happened throughout his years with the dolphins – from the discovery of the undersea world to his recovery here on the beach – had happened in the blinking of an eye, or perhaps the length of time that it had taken the sun to move from the center of the sky to the horizon.

Timmy might have shaken off this sensation had it not filled him with a foreboding that there wasn't much time left – if he wanted to see the dolphins more clearly, to touch their skin and, once again, bathe in the love that they had given him for so many years, he had to act now, before they moved off to another section of the reef or even out to sea again – and if he didn't act now, he would be forced to consign them along with his Grandpa and everything else to his memories, memories that could only be imperfectly seen and never touched or held or caressed. Maybe this was one of the greatest differences between life in the water and life on land -- in the water, time stretched out endlessly and one's memories were as vivid as life itself, while on land time was short and what had passed away could only be possessed partially and only for a short time in one's mind. Maybe this was nonsense; maybe the dolphins and his Grandpa were the only differences between life in the water and life on land. Timmy glanced around him, because the strange barks and squeals were coming back. They sounds were louder and more insistent now, and while he was certain that these sounds were not the sounds of the dolphins, he still couldn't identify them or make sense of what they were trying to convey, if they were trying to convey anything at all.

Timmy had to slip beneath the surface of the water one last time. Suspending himself between the surface and the bottom, he looked around at what now seemed to be an alien, hostile world, a place where he no longer belonged. The water was cool and unpleasant, and as he allowed himself to sink to the bottom where he rested on his back and gazed up at the shimmering surface of the water, he couldn't help thinking that he had come to the end of something, perhaps many things. Gazing at the surface, with its sparkling diamonds of light floating beyond reach, he noticed that the clouds were gone and that the sky was no longer red but blue. He was surprised over these changes, and he was beginning to think that the sky, like time itself, followed its own rules, which were incomprehensible to everything but the sky and time. At least, the birds swooning overhead were predictable, which provided some comfort in a world that was increasingly uncomfortable and alien. Timmy, despite all his efforts, felt alone both on land and in the water -- no place seemed to welcome him and no one in either world wholly embraced him or sought him out; even the others, who must have been aware of his presence, were now keeping their distance, leaving him floating with nothing but the birds overhead, silently moving from one part of the sky to the other, to remind him that he was alive.

For a short while, Timmy was again engulfed by a muffled silence, as if he had either lost his hearing or sound itself had disappeared, at least from the water. Unlike the last time, this time it was a strangely pleasant sensation. But after a few moments of yielding to the warm nothingness that surrounded him, he noticed something in the distance, small, barely perceptible bits of sound that resembled the gibberish that he had left behind while his head was still above the surface. He strained his ears as the sounds grew louder, but after a few moments he began to wonder if the sounds were simply the echoes of waves splashing overhead and crashing against distant rocks. It certainly made sense, and yet as the sounds continued to increase in volume, it became clear that they could not be caused solely by the action of water, if only because they lacked the regularity of the ocean's movements, which pounded against the shore like the ticking of a clock. For a brief moment, Timmy also wondered if the sounds could have been emanating from the dolphins, perhaps as a way to communicate with him, and yet even this didn't seem to be a satisfying answer because they were suddenly no where to be seen and, furthermore, some of the noise (rounded, song-like utterances) were uncharacteristic of the sounds that dolphins made. But as the noise became louder and more insistent, something almost primordial rose within him, a sensation that the sounds, whatever they were and whatever their origins, were meant for him. Memories of his Grandpa and home suddenly came to him, and he longed to go home to be among the people and things he loved.

Timmy would have breached the surface of the water to locate the origin of the noise, which was becoming louder and more insistent, but for some reason he couldn't move his arms and legs – he was unable to do anything but stare up at a sparkling, empty sky.

"My God," she was screaming. "My God, do you hear me?"

"For God's sake," a man's voice called out, although not in response to anything the woman was saying. "For God's sake…"

"Do something."

"Is there anything near…"

"For God's sake, Bob, don't worry about your shoes. Go out there and get him!"

The man's voice was suddenly silent, but the woman's voice was still insistent.

"It's not that deep, you fool. Grab his arms and legs and pull him out. For God's sake…"

"If it wasn't for that old fool…," the man finally retorted, his voice breathless and fading.

Timmy wanted to reach out to the shadow that was now at the edge of his sight, but his body still didn't obey his mind and he doubted that he could have touched it even had he been able to move. There was nothing ominous about the shadow, however, even though it continued to grow and was soon dominating nearly his entire field of vision. In the darkness that was beginning to swallow him there was still light, bright crystalline rays of sunlight that appeared at the edges of the shadow, trying to make their way past the shadow to tell him something. Something very important, something perhaps even crucial to life itself…but what? What? Was he too young to understand even this?

XXVII

In the darkness, Timmy could once again see his friends and his school, as well as his teachers and the rooms that served as classrooms and playrooms. He could see the school yard, with its old swings and slides and the weeds that grew on the edges of virtually everything, including the swing sets, the tarmac, and the school building itself, which he understood to be an old building, older than either his father or his mother. And he could also see his house and his bedroom, and all the toys, the books, and clothes that somehow defined both his living spaces and his being. It was all so vivid that he could see himself reaching under his bed for his dolphin book, spreading the wide covers, and turning page after page filled with wondrous pictures of dolphins swimming, playing, eating, and simply living. He could still feel the weight of the book, which because of its size was about as heavy as anything that he owned. Timmy longed to be back in the human world, even if he were a burden to his mom, even if he were never again allowed to see the water or even dolphins. Despite his love for the great mammals, he would have sacrificed them for one last chance to step foot on hard ground, to see his world again.

Timmy watched helplessly as the shadow seemed to get closer and then dip into the water, lifting him toward the surface where the sun's bright rays began to fade into complete darkness. For a brief second, he thought that he could see Bob's face in the shadow, his jaw set and his hair wet and disheveled; but as soon as Timmy breached the surface, all he could see was his Grandpa's smiling face as he pulled him to his chest and cradled him as if he were still a child.

- - -))) - -)) – ((- - (((- - -

www.ingramcontent.com/pod-product-compliance
Lightning Source LLC
Chambersburg PA
CBHW071402170626
46811CB00003B/1224